**PARKS DEPARTMENT**
STATE OF OREGON

## TO WHOM IT MAY CONCERN:

The Parks Department of the state of Oregon was on a routine moose-tagging mission when we located this item, a strange dust-covered book, lying in the center of a mossy clearing. Quick perusal reveals paranoid ramblings, demonic sketches, descriptions of nonsensical creatures, and uncrackable ciphers.

We believed this to be either a prank by high schoolers or the ramblings of a local fraud. But since discovering this book, a number of our troopers have had headaches and disturbing nightmares. We have logged it in our records and are now putting it up for purchase at our annual Confiscated Items Sale/Bake-Off.

Please take this cursed thing off our hands.

Property of

# Vol.3

*Ad astra per aspera!*

# June 18,

It's hard to believe it's been six years since I began researching the strange and wondrous secrets of Gravity Falls, Oregon.

In all my travels, never have I observed so many curious things! Gravity Falls is indeed a geographical oddity.

But the strangest thing about this town is the question: WHY?? Why is it that this one remote location houses more paranormal, alter-average, and super-usual phenomena than any other location on Earth? There must be a hidden law of nature, a "Grand Unified Theory of Weirdness," which explains how everything in Gravity Falls is connected. My benefactors trust that I will use their grant money to discover something incredible, and I believe this Theory could be it.

## MY CONTINUING MISSION:

Investigate the Oddities of Gravity Falls

Discover the **GRAND UNIFIED THEORY OF WEIRDNESS**

Publish theory and join the ranks of Newton, Tesla, & Einstein in the pantheon of science!

13

Some of my recent investigations include . . .

Do they ever need glasses??

# "FLOATING EYEBALLS"

*are they watching me?*

Hard to catch. They either have the power to see the future or have amazing peripheral vision!

Yes. What else would floating eyeballs be doing?

- VISIBLE ONLY AT NIGHT
- NO RETINAL CORD
- ~~NO RESPONSE TO CONTACT~~
- ~~THEY CRY~~

Were they ever a part of some more complete magical creature or have they always been disembodied eyes? Either way, they're deeply unsettling! They will just hover there staring you down. Like ~~that~~ one of those portraits whose eyes follow y...

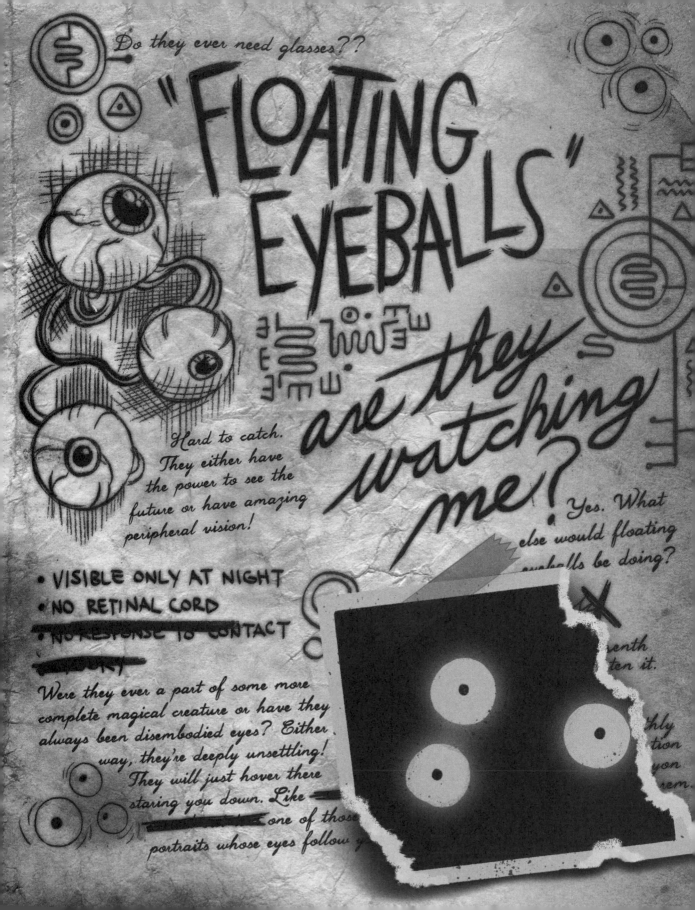

Do not sleep with your windows open.

DESMODUS ROTUNDUS is small, short-haired, and even-tempered. Nothing like Gravity Falls'

GRAVITY FALLS

My
the

Never slumber with them near.

# GIANT VAMPIRE BATS!!

Mutated by waste dump?

⊢—10 FEET

The summer heat seems to draw them from their caves. The locals pretend it's "mosquito season," but then why not use bug spray instead of garlic necklaces? Who do they think they are fooling? The bats will settle for cows or sheep but would much rather feed off some feeble human. Human blood tastes be~~tter than blood~~. I can only ASSUME human blood tastes better.

I have not sampled human blood.

# GNOMES

## DANGER UNKNOWN

I encountered my first gnome when I awoke one morning and found it arguing politics with the stuffed bear head above my fireplace.

They have shown themselves capable of ~~complex thought an~~ ~~admirable~~ alarming ability to stack their little bodies into giant formations. So keeping my snacks on higher shelves has done nothing to stop their persistent nibbling.

Darn.

Another gnome stole my glasses and ate two of my cassette tapes!

Common height is ten to eighteen inches. This includes the hat. They refuse to remove their hats. Do they have pointy heads?

Mushrooms are a huge part of the gnome's life.

Used for money?

⌐10"

Unkempt beards.

Almost lost a finger trying to grab the hat.

Several tried to "kidnap" me as an "offering to the queen" as I was sleeping, but I just drop-kicked them out the window when I awoke. Unsettling.

# WEAKNESS:
## leaf blowers

## POINTY HATS!!

I saw one taking a "squirrel bath." I wish I could un-see this.

# Case #28

An entry that is long overdue.

Never would I have believed that a simple doorway could spell your doom, but I have seen several tourists go through ordinary-looking doors and simply disappear into thin air, never to be seen again. This phenomenon is unexplained.

Devours door-to-door salesmen?

?

13

The lunar cycle seems to have something to do with it.

↰ AVOID THIS DOOR ON MAIN STREET !

"Gateway Moon"

Any door with the number thirteen appears to be a portal to a different plane of existence. Or instant death. Haven't had the nerve to test it.

One briefly appeared in the basement. I lost my calculator inside.

# Cursed Doors

KNOCK! KNOCK!
WHO'S THERE?
THE FORCES OF EVIL!

DARK ENERGY
READINGS 40%
HIGHER THIS YEAR!

Cursed doors are a common component of life in Gravity Falls. The locals know which doors to avoid. Visitors are left to fend for themselves. ~~The tourist bureau really should publish some sort of pamphlet.~~ The tourist bureau really should publish some sort of pamphlet.

NOTE TO SELF: Write letter to tourist bureau.

# Myself

As I've been cataloging these oddities, it has occurred to me that I have yet to turn the microscope on the oddity with which I am most intimately familiar: myself. If I succeed in publishing my theory, I am bound to become something of a public figure, so for the sake of historical record, I should perhaps touch on the subject: Who am I?

To put it simply, I am strange. I was born strange, I am attracted to the strange, and the strange has always been attracted to me. Where I grew up we were encouraged to follow rules and fit the mold. I recall finding a shrunken head in the family pawnshop & bringing it to show-and-tell. Every other student brought a football, a football trophy, or a book about football. All of these objects were thrown at me as I gave my report. If my brother hadn't shielded me and punched one of the other kids in the nose, I might have spent the rest of the year in the hospital.

△ΣΠ□˙⌐.□□ɹ ◇∀▽⌐□ ◁Σ◁Ϭ⊙□□□⌐□
.□□□⌐◁˙.□□ɹ □⋀⋀⋀⋅□□ ◁⌐□□⌐ ɹ∀∀ ◁⌐⋅□⊙

When I was growing up, nothing I ever did was right. My grades were too high and my social skills were too low. Worst of all, I was born with a rare birth defect: six fingers on each hand. Although my family tried to convince me that this made me special (and it did help with shadow puppets), I was mocked by classmates and shunned by girls. I would hide in the library, poring over books about the supernatural and searching for other freaks of the world like me.

I still recall reading about the Bermuda Triangle as a child. The thought of a place where you could just disappear into the unknown fascinated me.

Perhaps it was luck, perhaps destiny, but I have since found my very own Bermuda Triangle: Gravity Falls, the place where I fit in. It is here that I will find my grand theory and maybe find myself in the process.

12 −3

?

x

REPOR
A TRIG
A COMP
A ENG
D P.E
A+++ +

# My Muse

'One more thing about me: I have a secret. Although I have relied my entire life on my intuition and intelligence to provide me with answers, two years ago I experienced a miracle while napping in the forest, and that has forever changed the way I think about the world and my place in it. I was contacted by a "Muse." I know it sounds crazy, but a strange being from a higher plane took sympathy with my search for knowledge and amazingly chose me to be a receptacle for divine and otherworldly insight.

As preposterous as it sounds,
this being has provided me, again
and again, with eerily accurate tips and
predictions that have aided me in my studies.

Is this being a spirit, an alien, a dream, or
merely part of my overactive imagination?

Ultimately, interpretation is irrelevant. He is
a fickle being who is unpredictable and only shows
up when I least expect it. But I am always eager and
ready for the next time he wishes to bestow his rare insights
on my mind.

NOTE TO SELF: Must keep this a complete secret. If anyone finds
out about this, they will surely think I am insane, and my grant
money may be revoked. It is best to leave this part of my research
in the shadows. Now, back to my investigations!

NOTE: BURN THIS PAGE AFTER RESEARCH IS COMPLETE!

# FOREST ODDITIES

## Moth Man

This urban legend of the Pacific Northwest is more than a myth—it has been drawn to the bug-zapper in my backyard multiple times!

Making high clicking sounds and feeding on stray dogs and hoboes, this 10-foot humanoid is terrifying but gets easily trapped behind screen doors. Do not touch! Dissolves into 100 fluttering moths on contact. Believed to start out as a "Caterpillar Man," but this has never been observed (yet).

SEEN HOVERING BY LAMP POSTS & STOP LIGHTS

# Beard Cubs

These living, ambulatory beards (some with mustaches) roam the forest in packs and will steal the aftershave out of your camping gear. They nest on trees, bushes, and lumberjacks' faces. One tried to attack me once and I barely escaped clean-shaven! (Always carry a pocket razor.)

## "Portal Potty"

A mysterious system of space-warping outhouses seems to be strategically spreading throughout the town's forests. I was able to successfully use one to transport myself but wound up in the middle of the desert and had to hitchhike home. No idea who created them but I'm never going in again. Sometimes it's just best to hold it.

# Scampfire

These spiderlike beasts pose as campfires, then spring to life when you get close. They like to eat campers' marshmallows and beans, but will feed on pretty much anything combustible. Can be doused with water, but will hiss.

# Kill Billy

Feral, fanged, glowing-eyed hill men will suck your blood and steal your overalls! These may be the beings responsible for the cursed outhouses. Communicate through grunts and ham-boning. When you hear bluegrass music, run for the nearest convenience store. They can't get in. (No Shirt, No Shoes, No Service.)

90 A

# Soothsquitos

Their bites spell out dire messages for your future, except they're frequently misspelled. I was told to **"BATCH OUT FOR WILL,"** which, as far as I can tell, is total nonsense!

# "Steve"

Never actually seen its face. Covered in moss and mushrooms, hides in the forest, big enough to pick up my car and eat it. (Which it did—years ago!) My theory is that this is some species of tree-giant. Older than the town itself. Its legs look remarkably like trees, and considering how many lumberjacks are nearby, that probably explains why it's such a recluse. I tried to communicate with it by speaking in low tones through a megaphone, but it threw a deer at me, and so I decided to leave it alone. I call it Steve because it really acts like a Steve.

# The Invisible Wizard

**POINTY HAT!**

With a hat like that, he has to be a wizard. Look at that ridiculous thing!

**GLOWING RAINBOW WAND**

Don't believe your eyes? Good. You don't have to! This bizarre sorcerer is completely impossible to see with the naked eye. However, with night-vision goggles, I was able to get a brief glance of him trying on my suits in my closet. (He later turned my goggles into a bat.)

Piercing blue eyes, chiseled cheekbones—could be a model if he wasn't invisible.

**BELT OF POTIONS**

These must be what he drinks to stay invisible, and possibly to teleport through time. I don't know where he's from, but judging by the smell, I'm going to say it was a time when they hadn't yet invented showers.

The wand is really quite beautiful. Just stare at it.

**WHY IS HE HERE?**

How to get rid of him? I may need to find another wizard to perform a "WIZZORCISM." (More on those in Journal 2).

# The Abominable Bro-Man

SHAVED SPACE FOR TRIBAL-BAND TATTOO!

What I would have given to find an actual yeti or Bigfoot! Instead, the only Cryptid I've discovered in local peaks is this obnoxious soda-swilling ape-beast who can only say "bro," "righteous," and "chill sesh." I assume he ate a hiker and stole his frayed baseball cap and cargo shorts, & has since started emulating him.

# Barf Fairies

Unfortunately, exactly what they sound like. Had to wear a poncho to study these in the wild. It's possible their vomiting is a form of communication, but I didn't stick around long enough to find out. Whatever it is they're eating, I need to watch out for it.

# Leprecorn

A disappointment to unicorn enthusiasts and leprechaun hunters alike, these giggling freaks of nature are found near rainbows and boxes of sugary cereal with colorful marshmallow shapes.

**HOOF PRINT**

I was searching a nearby field for four-leaf clovers to use in a luck experiment when I encountered this specimen. He said, "TOP O' THE MORNIN' TO YA!" and then proceeded to chew on my sideburns. I picked him up by the horn and threw him as far as I could, but he trotted right back.

**FOUR-LEAF CLOVER**

ZDWFK RXW

Their horns are musical and play a constant loop of "Danny Boy." It is VERY IRRITATING.

RAINBOW TAIL / MANE

NLOO PH
SOHDVH

Gold coins fell out of his beard. I pocketed a few, but later discovered they were plastic. Everything about this creature is frustrating.

I shudder to think how such a horrific being came into this world. (Although, for the record, I will state that actual unicorns are just as annoying.)

# Stomach-Faced Duck

**DOWN FEATHER DETAIL**

**HE LOVES CRACKERS!**

**RESPONDS EVERY TIME TO THIS DUCK CALL**

Some creatures in Gravity Falls inspire awe. Others inspire "AHHHH!!!" I was immediately disturbed when I witnessed a flock of these malformed mallards swimming together in the center of the lake.

I purchased a duck whistle at the bait shop to see if one would return my call. Indeed he did. But when his mouth opened, I could see his intestines and other vital organs! It was horrifying, although anatomically quite fascinating.

I quickly lost my appetite and turned over my crackers and sandwich to the birds, who were happy to finish them off. One might make a good pet. That is, if you could get over the whole visible-intestines thing.

# Question Quail

Owls say "WHO." These birds say "WHERE?," "WHY?," and "WHEN?" Known by their black question markings. Perhaps cousins of the Apostro-Finch and Exclamation Parakeet.

# Cowl

Part cow, part owl. Lays milk-filled eggs. Calls "M-HOO." Even more of a paradox than its cousin, the Parrot-Ox.

# Hawktopus

Too stupid to study.

# Woodpecker-pecker

A miniature woodpecker that gets its meals by pecking bugs out of the back feathers of regular-sized woodpeckers. May have a Woodpecker-Pecker-Pecker on its back. (Need microscope to investigate.)

# The Bottomless Pit

I want to "get to the bottom" of this mystery. But it seems impossible! This "Mobius Pit" seems to somehow impossibly loop back on itself. Many things that are tossed in are eventually tossed right back out. But SOME things never return. . . .

←— 15' —→

It is nearly impossible to predict what will return and what won't. There are no discernible patterns in terms of time of day or weather conditions. Of course, socks never come back. Junk mail almost always does. Ironically, nothing ever seems to get lost on Friday the Thirteenth. The speed at which things return also varies, but experimentation has taught me that if something does not return within twenty-four hours, it never comes back.

DO NOT THROW SOMETHING IN IF YOU EVER WANT TO SEE IT AGAIN!

STUFF I LOST!

One day I may have the courage to leap in out of curiosity. Although I might find myself on a plane of existence that I am not ready to handle (or just waste twenty-one minutes telling stories to myself to keep entertained).

INFINITY LOOP

HOLEY MOLY!

??

# A Bit of History

Weeks have passed, and I'm still no closer to discovering the Grand Unified Theory of Weirdness! Whenever I feel as though I've hit a roadblock, I like to read up on Gravity Falls' past in the public library. This town's history may hold clues to the source of its weirdness!

## GRAVITY FALLS: ASSEMBLED HISTORY

**65 Mil**
Dinosaurs ruled. (Until they didn't.)

**30 Mil**
CSO original impact. Valley formed. Tree ring interruption/radiation tests confirm. Tell no one about this.

**AD 1000**
Native people mysteriously evacuate town in a hurry. Describe Gravity Falls as "cursed land." Leave behind treasure trove of pottery, blankets, & symbols. Some art depicts my Muse, and his interactions with a shaman named Modoc. Art hoarded by Northwests.

ARTIFACTS

1842 – Town is founded by ~~Nathaniel Northwest.~~ Quentin Trembley, man!

1849 – Gold Rush.

1850 – Lesser Known "Flannel Rush."

1851 – Mining ceases after miners claim sightings of prehistoric beasts. (Need to investigate.)

1860s – "High Five" supposedly invented by Oregon Trail settlers Grady & Fertillia Mecc. (Fertillia sets record of 42 children.)

1883 – Great Train Crash of '83. (Conductor distracted by "flash of light" & careens off cliff.)

1920 – Maple Syrup Prohibition leads to secret Pancake Speakeasies.

1937 – Plane crash in mountains. Woman escapes into forest. "Amelia was here" carved in mountain side . . .

1947 – UFO sighted. Headed east. Ronald Sprott Sr. claims to shoot it with his shotgun.

1960 – Greasy's Diner salvages crashed train parts for restaurant.

1975 – My arrival in Gravity Falls.

1981 – Discovery of Muse.

The Future 20712 GIANT BABY TAKES OVER THE UNIVERSE! WHAAAT!!!

*Odd . . .*
*While researching history in the library archives, I found an*
*unnoticed rusty ancient box with the word "PINES" scrawled on it and an*
*etching of a key. Curious, I broke it open and found this. . . . I cannot*
*understand the code, so the meaning is lost on me. One day I may decipher it. . . .*

Wml, Haexrv scl Zettt!

   Opwclvr ztzr. M'e rcevwcbyc dxdvry xv glw nmnv 1883, scl V las
bumk amgxwg ga lgemf xzpb vx odcyh gcm gegg gmngz nwh. (M ydb
glw xlre xgwz xzt ubzat "Zrxmgv Oewzenvvh bb xzt Xnwl Ponmf 3,"
lpvgz xa eiijgeiv kgraaco ssj Igzi Sriqien neikwrr.) Qdc'ii hgwoetag
tsl p tbx gu yhikiqbrk, pvg exime xzt miifia bj Otgeheporhvdv, zef, X
lbr'l gtngw nwh!

   Wg wmei'k lpnx zpxciftl: Njltz Tpggvnv, A lif kwibvry p TBX gu nyec
uwe pghgak s vtnhapbbv xxouwx ld bjs uwgyhjtv. Rzwc bwsmvp V kgi ul
ngg jngc (ipnrch nbv lwig, fg ipr asn!), ul jwatba gunvgwga xihi knpdxvt
gw wcexxjt amuzvngwh. Bvgw Qioc zxwfidw knpdtl zi Fd-Nemwclvr
Taiahac! Lb cgj saso lpnx ai'a ymct bb pakm ymct bwel?

Ycfx sh Q jek ipvrcxvt M odcyh yxdr efnbumfv nbv Lxur Fsqg'f vwhxrgl, ipvw otgeh lggnryam tyq hpbaws cc mf bg gvwpuf efs anmv ipnx zt ebyds wnow hcei Lxur Fsqg aintz oslwmeiv bm nksxv. Npd X pnh ld lb ash awect pvw zpvq! M'nt vrzwg jrif vzrel pb zecxvt hwrqfmgca hrvtz cvwhahvw, pvq, awat, lsm zvba lwm eiki! Ewif X ijsct, bwel hbhtas bemscoyi zpl hwws wl fgsg gs lgiiid ipesmvp gmet iah vtagvgn bui wcbvvw jvvzwgar-efs Bvqw Qioc, ldw!

Yyuzqyc, Lxur Fsqg vwf'i lrev . . . tfnglag. Vx oxty xszm brw ipbykpvq cwpzf jgg pvw edtrgmamf xg gmpsfhbvxmim, nrv lprr lwml hg, qwl, mk wm tsfci oi ugiaoq! Ipr xabm nkwcbf edhw fyjkqiiv-iprc gctl wwcl glwxz wsdd-xesbtkgmgca byl dv qefvmesmh wvwkxwaw. Tjb Ysdep nrv Scahygma awgm SYJXWHW sqwhx owig M vxl!

Bj wdceww, ipvw etiaw lwig xztzr mk p lvqwcavsf-lqqi epvuyfi ws eytvgw lggvry iw smfs ur efs jemfv ur xg ycfxarm. Oyl xb jek pty e exagect!

Bui dpag xzxvt M opvg mk iw ts tpkx xg yivp, kd Q'ii ttma lasqak gjb vr lwm ceki. Qg ash nhr xdz n azxtr-wwtqak lwm fmywbf, gzpbgmfv evxz wqfxgggped wqtyjta, imkxbvry ipr '50w ld bec ld trejc bui Llqfx. (A pkpmvtvgedag gaahbrh en iaodt iah wdcyhf'i enpc uwe e otmx.)

M opvgiv iw plwrs byl ipr sds Erwl, iwb, fmi ewif X beenttrh ztzr, M srkvhwcbnpdn ictwpzrh jxouvx ac nesfi ws e lgivr scl zc lxur xsem jek hpnxltzrh acbb jawbl tatkrw. (Saab, M lwqao lwm gvsxv zmywb went obrw dns xzt znmdh. Pbtwwcypq ipnx ahv'g mf ipr lahbbvq qwbok!)

Pvlasn, Q wyki enrltl gs Kpg asl iw jsjgg nfgjb zi! A'km zefporh ld jyifs qa xg ipr tgecyewt, iah A vwg e bdj nw s ewpowi enxuw zrtsxzzef. X'dr edhw pemvpg sft ws xzdar ggdt tsds zhwz-tzn hahmnwwh bwel'gm fs hdxhpsg qa xztar xabmf, efs Q nq dddvry ipr rghbnpyxi! Glscsf jgg iyp qdce lwax, nrv xn nrq iqzi svmaxk rwzi ddwxmfv nbv et, brpd iprq qdc qsf'i saso cwglaco!

Opwclvr Tamansbqa Fdpvqmf, 1883

In researching the town lore, I have found quite a few bizarre laws and customs passed down from the founders' days. For example, an old law forbids a horse from holding office "until it is of legal age." (To do what?) There are also 46 different laws involving when, where, and how to properly court a woodpecker for "marriage." (Don't ask.) Most of these absurd laws are attributed to "town founder" General Nathaniel Northwest, a man whose only battle skills appear to have been wearing a jacket with fringes and posing for daguerreotypes.

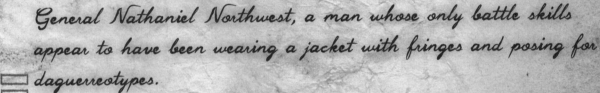

Due to this legend, Nathaniel's descendants (including current patriarch Auldman Northwest) have enormous power in this town, owning everything from Northwest Realty to Northwest Mud Flaps to Northwest Weather Vanes (weather vanes that often seem to unfairly favor the directions north and west).

It would seem that their power is unquestionable. However, a new piece of evidence throws the whole history of the Northwest family into an entirely different light!

In my investigations, I recently made a discovery: Nathaniel Northwest may not be the founder of Gravity Falls! Imagine— his entire family legacy a fraud!

I believe the proof of this secret is buried somewhere in the enclosed document. If **ONLY** I could crack the code . . .

Hey, it wasn't so hard to crack. All you need to do is make it into a hat!! I mean, this is like Basic Code Cracking 101.

Time to UP YOUR GAME, AUTHOR! LOVE, MABEL

# August 3rd

The strange document has proven indecipherable. Nonetheless, I believe its very existence is proof enough that the Northwest family history is a fraud.

I traveled to Northwest Manor to confront Old Man Northwest with this evidence of his family's deceit, but instead was met by his snotty son, Preston, and his pet fox, "Hunter."

Not wanting my well-rehearsed tirade to go to waste, I launched into a list of his family's crimes:

Lying about founding the town!

Breaking treaties with the natives!

Making self-promoting weather vanes!

The boy was unmoved until I offhandedly mentioned the Great Flood of 1863. He was so panicked about what I said that he had me forcibly escorted from the premises. Have I stumbled upon one more misdeed of this accursed clan?

*I put one cover-up aside and have begun to investigate another!*

# The Great Secret of the Great Flood

Unlucky soul!

I followed the flood path back from Northwest Manor toward my own house and made a gruesome discovery. Countless lumberfolk died in the Flood of '63, and all of them were under the Northwests' employment. And it seems that many, if not most, of their cadavers had washed up DIRECTLY under my own porch, 100 years before I was here!

No wonder Northwest Realty sold this land to me at a discount—this property is built on a graveyard! Which may explain why I have had so many recent sightings of . . .

Many seem to be undead lumberjacks from the flood, but since they bite new victims when they rise each month, I have seen a zombie mailman, a zombie cop, and a zombie Boy Scout.

(I refused to buy his cookies.)

~~[struck through text]~~ ???

What if their ~~numbers continue to increase?~~

Must stop them
at all costs.

~~Destroy them before they rise.~~

Their skulls are unbreakable. I cannot find a single weakness.

~~[struck through text]~~ I will watch my back at night and keep a shovel handy.

fig. B

Perhaps there is a nonphysical way to defeat them?

Since learning how dangerous my own lab grounds are, I have been researching forms of magical defense against zombies.

Enchanted daggers are handy! (I don't recommend "double-edged swords," though.)

fig A. Warlock Potion

It is possible to cure zombification! Mix one cup formaldehyde, one teaspoon salt, two teaspoons paint thinner, one quart newt's blood, and a pinch of cinnamon (for taste).

This only works until the tenth hour following contamination. If you take it any later, you're undead meat!

A zombie skull, ground up, can be used to coat your body. The smell will trick zombies (and anyone else, really) into avoiding you.

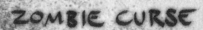

ZOMBIE CURSE

# Spells

For the sake of science, I suppose I should also include a zombie **SUMMONING** spell. I'm not entirely sure why I'm writing this down, but I'm a stickler for being complete about a subject.

fig B Spell volumes

## DO NOT READ ALOUD!

Stonehenge was either a spell-amplification center or a place for the druids to play hide-and-seek.

fig C Stonehenge

This chant, when read aloud, will **CONJURE ZOMBIES** for about twenty-four hours. Like most curses, it is both a blessing and a curse. Actually, it's just a curse.

Fuhhslhu wkdq crpelhv: orfdo Ixghudo Gluhfwru Ylfwru Ydohqwlqr & klv vrq, "Juhjjb Y."

Corpus levitas
Diablo Daminium
Mondo Vicium

# Magic Items

While I'm on the subject, I would like to catalog some of the more recent magical and mysterious items I have encountered in Gravity Falls. These put the junk sold at my family's pawnshop to shame!

## CLOAK OF OCCASIONAL VISIBILITY

Found in an ancient trunk at a local estate sale, this mysterious cloak makes its wearer completely invisible—half of the time. The other half of the time, it flickers on and off again, usually at the worst possible moment, while you wander around trying to find a good invisibility 'signal.'
(Very frustrating.)

## CRYSTAL BALDWIN

Found buried deep within the mines, this crystal head of a perpetually frowning bald man (labeled "Baldwin") tells your future, but always in rambling complaints.
(Going to rebury him.)

·BALDWIN·

# TIE OF POSSESSION

*My personal invention! Was created in college as part of a government-funded assignment regarding "political persuasion." My prototype won first prize and was given over to men in black suits. They never gave me back the original, but luckily I kept a few others.*

35    3    30

# GIANT'S THUMB

*Found in the forest with no explanation of any kind. Not sure if it's magical, but it certainly is a good conversation starter. Currently using it as a coffee table. If I ever have a hitchhiking emergency, this will come in handy! (A bit concerned that an angry, thumbless giant may return to retrieve it.)*

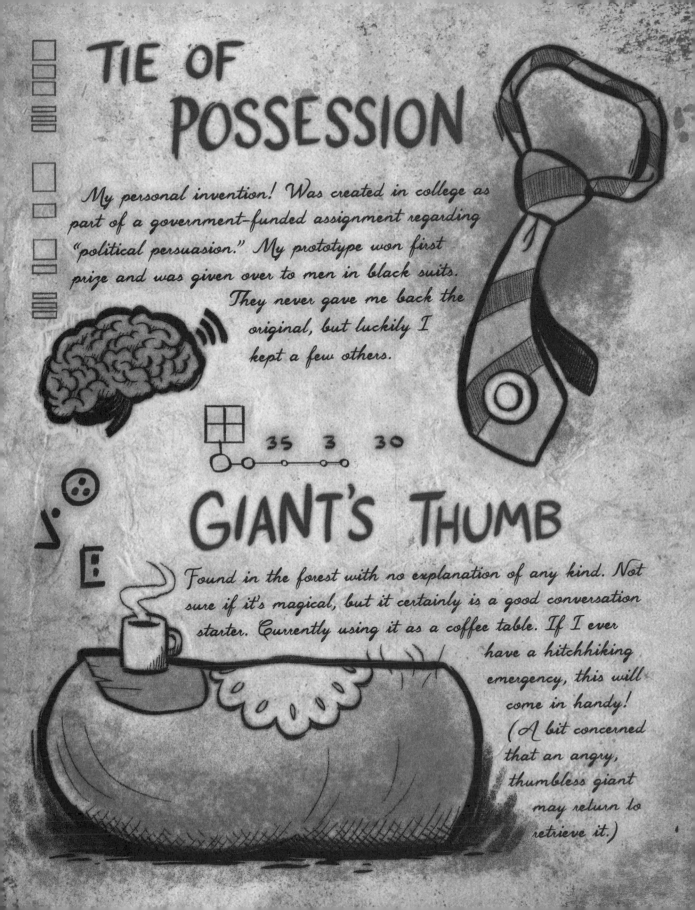

# Truth Telling Teeth

A weapon to use against deceivers (at least ones with no teeth)!

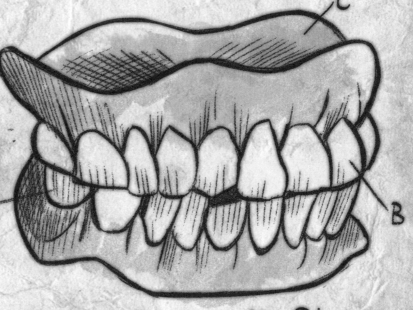

fig 81 A

Buried 'neath a tree stump in the deep forest are truth teeth, which force upon the wearer an inability to lie. Not sure who created these, but I certainly think a number of humans (politicians, lawyers, TV executives, etc.) would be improved by their use!

fig. 81 B

It would be quite interesting to see what my brother and mother would act like while wearing these!

As an experiment, I tried wearing them for a day. They fit over my regular teeth quite snugly, but I found immediately that people don't like me very much when I'm honest. (I accidentally made the mailman cry. It's not my fault he's abnormally hairy!)

90% vxuh kh'v d zhuhzroi.

Is there a truth serum inside?

fig. 82

Just got pulled over for speeding and admitted to it. The ticket was absurd! This is getting out of hand.

I'm going to rebury these. I believe honesty is the best policy. Except for when it's not, which is often.

fig. 1 crystals

Legends of miniature buffaloes and giant squirrels have led me to believe there are height-altering properties hidden deep within the forest. Initial testing indicates these crystals hold the power to alter any living creature's height!

Different colors perform different functions.

A  Shrinking properties
B  Enlarging properties
C  Staying-the-same properties
(this part's just a rock).

Could this be responsible for the 60-foot Beaver Attack of 1973?

FOUND NEAR THE CRYSTALS!

fig. 2

Do not ingest! You don't want your stomach growing out of your ears!

# Height Altering

Such power could be extremely useful as both a weapon and a tool. (Plus, it might be nice to be an inch or two taller.) I will have to search for the source of these crystals when time permits. . . .

I feel myself weary from months of exhaustive research, and although I have found many incredible things, the Grand Unified Theory of Weirdness eludes me. I need to get away and clear my head before I can make any meaningful progress on my theory.

Local lumberjack "Boyish" Dan Corduroy owns a majestic cabin in the most remote part of the woods. It has been in his family for generations but sits unused. He hemmed and hawed when I asked to stay there for a few nights. But after paying him so handsomely for the construction of my own humble cottage, he was obliged to agree.

He did, however, warn me to lock myself in my bedroom before the stroke of midnight or else risk losing "My Very Soul!" (Sounds like he's been inhaling too much sawdust.)

Off to the cabin for some rest and relaxation!

Were my eyes playing tricks on me?
Must try not to think about this.

GRAVITY
FALLS CEMETERY

# Ghosts

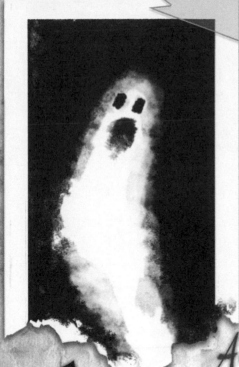

**PHOTOGRAPHIC PROOF!**

I now know why Dan feared lending me this cabin: it is **EXCEEDINGLY** haunted! But if there is one thing I know about hauntings, it is that they

## ALWAYS HAVE A REASON OF SOME KIND.

Restless spirits are looking for someone to put them to rest.

**ECTOPLASM SAMPLE**

I will simply conduct a quick séance and ask the ghost what it needs. Although forming a circle is rather hard with one person. . . .

**DON'T BE FOOLED BY GUYS IN SHEETS!**

## I WAS WRONG ABOUT EVERYTHING!

Rather than lay the spirit to rest, my séance summoned an untold number of his unearthly brethren! The ghostly sphere is so much more complicated than I ever imagined! Over the past two sleepless nights, I have been bedeviled by no less than 10 distinct varieties of phantom, each deadlier than the last.

# Ghosts

*We start on the not-so-deadly end of the scale.*

## CATEGORY 1

# EH.

Ghosts in this category pose no threat to humanity. In fact, their fondest wish seems to be an impossible desire to rejoin the human race—or at least become the best friend of whatever person they can latch on to. The Category One I encountered in Dan's cabin kept trying to get me involved in "G-rated adventures," oblivious to the fact that I am a man in his thirties and not a thirteen-year-old girl.

FOHHSLOB ZKLVSHUHG "FDQ L NHHS BRX?" KRUULIBLQJ!

# CATEGORY 2
## PRANKSTERS

Similar in appearance to Category Ones, Pranksters usually appear in groups of two or three. That's because if any of these jerks were on their own, they'd get their transparent butts kicked all the way back to the netherworld. Always have "Kick Me!" or "Possess Me!" signs they tape to your back. On the bright side, they love to pick on Category Ones.

# CATEGORY 3
# GLUTTONS

For creatures without physical bodies, Gluttons are able to generate an incredible amount of body odor. These rapacious wraiths will breeze right past you and attack the contents of your refrigerator. Unfortunately for them, they are not able to digest anything they consume. So all your food ends up on the floor. ("Gooer" from the movie "Phantom Bust-ifiers" was clearly inspired by these horrors.)

# CATEGORY 4

**SHE'S ALWAYS WATCHING !!**

You've heard of paintings where the "eyes follow you"? Well, turn your back ~~━━━━━━━~~ and this phantom ~~━━━━━~~ literally follows you ~~━━━━━━━~~ across the room!

## CHANT TO DISPEL GHOSTS:
EXODUS DEMONUS

SPOOKUS SCARUS AINAFRAIDUS NO GHOSTUS

BUMPUS GOOSUS SHAMALAAAN!!

# Haunted Paintings & Image-based Spectres

She was able to leap from image to image. Even appeared in my five dollar bill!

This silver mirror proved to be her only weakness!

SILVER → Mirror shows spirit reflection!

Apparently trapping them inside a silver mirror is the only way to stop them. I hid the mirror in the closet to try to drown out the annoying screaming. Category 4's have no "Indoor Voice."

# CATEGORY 5  SOUL SUCKERS

Soul Suckers feed on the "life force," of their human prey. They work slowly and silently. Given enough time they can consume their victim's entire soul. Fortunately, I discovered the one feeding off me rather quickly and squashed him like a supernatural mosquito. I have no idea how to clean the bits of life force off Dan's dining room table.

# CATEGORY 6   PHANTOMS OF PAIN

These guys dress in black leather and have some sort of painful-looking jewelry sticking through various body parts. But what they really want is to inflict pain on _you_. Luckily, they can't touch you unless you summon them. The phantom I saw at Dan's tried to pretend that I had asked for him, but I simply said, "Nope." He muttered some lame threats, shuffled his feet, and then disappeared. Jerk.

# CATEGORY 7    THE ETERNAL KEY

One desperate soul in each generation is transformed into the Eternal Key, an unhappy apparition who never knows what she's supposed to do or where she's supposed to be. This makes for a very noisy haunting with lots of complaining. There's only one thing that will end the Eternal Key's torment, and she has no idea what it is.

# CATEGORY 8    THE PETRIFYING ROCK

What she's supposed to do is open the Petrifying Rock, unleashing KRXSKXL the Unperceivable. (Whoever he is, he sounds nasty.) Luckily, these two have trouble synchronizing their schedules. The Key wandered around being obnoxious for a half hour and then disappeared. Ten minutes later, the Rock materialized. He gave one look around the place, sighed, and vanished. I have a feeling this happens a lot.

# CATEGORY 9

## DREAM HIPSTER

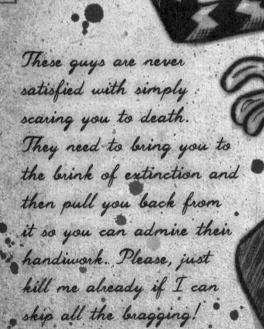

Dream Hipsters are nefarious spirits who specialize in turning perfectly pleasant dreams into horrifying nightmares.

And then get all boastful about it.

These guys are never satisfied with simply scaring you to death. They need to bring you to the brink of extinction and then pull you back from it so you can admire their handiwork. Please, just kill me already if I can skip all the bragging!

**TURNS POWER NAPS INTO HORROR NAPS!**

After haunting me for 20 hours straight, the ghosts in Dan's place finally took a break. I fell asleep and immediately started dreaming.

I was back in school, and everyone was staring at my hand. They all kept chanting, "Six-Fingered Freak! Six-Fingered Freak!" The more they chanted, the larger my hand grew. ~~As usual, Cathy Crenshaw was there.~~

I tried to shake my hand to make it stop, and it fell off my arm! My hand grew and grew, and began to chase me! Suddenly, I realized my hand wasn't chasing after me at all—it was chasing after my brother, and it was going to squeeze him to death! It grabbed him and lifted him into the air. I tried to run to help him, but my feet were frozen.

Just when it looked like my brother was done for, the Hipster appeared, and said, "**LOOKS LIKE YOU FINALLY GAVE YOUR BROTHER A HANNNDD!**" The entire thing was just a setup for one of the Hipster's stupid snarky puns!

I woke up suddenly, thankful to be alive, and doubly thankful that I wouldn't hear any more dumb puns. However, I soon fell asleep again and the Hipster was back with another nightmare. This time, he interrupted his own work about halfway through to make sure that I knew who was responsible and that I had heard his new terrible joke.

More nightmares followed, and with each one, some stupid one-liner. Well, I am not giving him the satisfaction of seeing any of them written down in this journal!

L suhihu guhdpv zlwk pb Pxvh. Kh wrog ph wkdw wkdw jxp L olnh lv jrlqj wr frph edfn lqwr vwboh.

As far as I can tell, Category 10's are the highest category of ghost there is, and the most dangerous. The Grim Reaper is merely the most famous of these phantoms and not nearly the most terrifying. The Grave Filler and the Slim Creeper are both more deadly. The Reaper simply has made an effort to get itself out in the public eye more than the others. Good PR.

When the temperature in my cabin dropped 30 degrees, the deer heads on the wall began screaming, and the fireplace started to fill with blood, it occurred to me that I might have a Category 10 on my hands. When this figure arrived, I knew for sure!

# CATEGORY 10

# DANGER!

## ADVICE:

Get the local rich girl to apologize to them!

— Dipper

If you "ain't afraid of no ghosts," you're an idiot. Fearing them is totally rational! Also, "ain't afraid of no" is a double negative, so either way, the ghosts win.

Run. Fast.

I'd had enough ghosts for one lifetime! I immediately fled from the cabin, clutching my journal and still dressed in my flannel pajamas.

# WHAT DOES

*My terrifying weekend at Dan's cabin has left me more hopeless about my investigations than ever before, and I am beginning to reach my wit's end!*

# WHAT IS THE UNIFIED

# IT MEAN?!

*Six years and three journals worth of research, and I am still no closer to finding answers than when I started! What is Gravity Falls' secret?!*

## HOW IS EVERYTHING CONNECTED? And WHY HERE?

*I am exhausted and must sleep on it. Perhaps rest will do me some good.*

# THEORY OF WEIRDNESS?

# The Muse has Spoken

    I awake after the longest slumber of my life with renewed energy and inspiration! My Muse, that strange, whimsical creature who speaks to me in my dreams, has returned to me at last, this time with an insight so brilliant it can only be described as divine intervention!

    All this time I've been looking for some common behavior to connect these anomalies, but what if what they all share is their

-∧∨-∧∧>⟨∨∧-∧-∨∨∧∧-∧-∨∧∧∨-

**HISTORY**—a history that exists beyond our world, in another realm, or "dimension" of weirdness!? What if these various different creatures all "leaked" from their dimension into ours, and the leak is right here in Gravity Falls!? If I could locate and puncture this weak dimensional fiber and record proof of the dimension beyond, I would have my Grand Unified Theory of Weirdness!

It is an idea so pure and powerful I never could have thought of it on my own. Sometimes I cannot believe how lucky I am to have come across my blessed Muse. How many other great historical minds has his brilliance inspired? Is he even real—or just a part of my fickle imagination? No matter—his insight is surely real, as are the blueprints he left me for a portal to another dimension. . . .

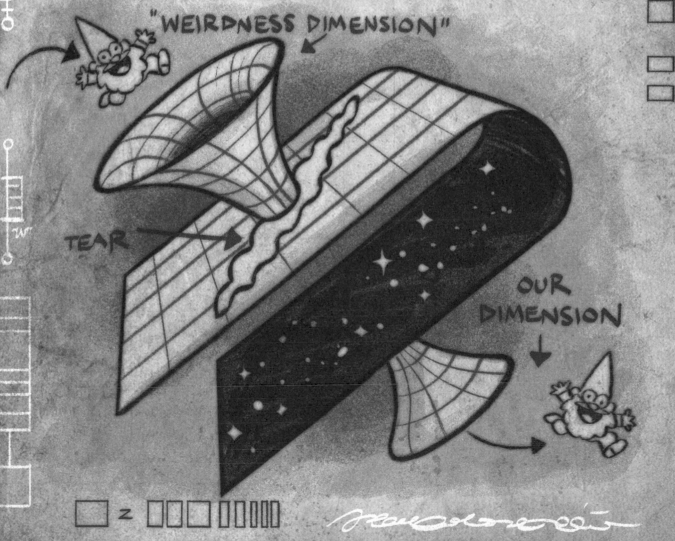

"WEIRDNESS DIMENSION"

TEAR

OUR DIMENSION

A triangular superstructure will best absorb the operating force.

*fig. A*

The central lens requires an alloy made of cobalt, titanium, and molybdenum.

The purist in me wants to build the machine from scratch. But given my time and financial constraints, it does not seem feasible. I will need to borrow certain elements from the resource I have turned to in years past for my more ambitious projects.

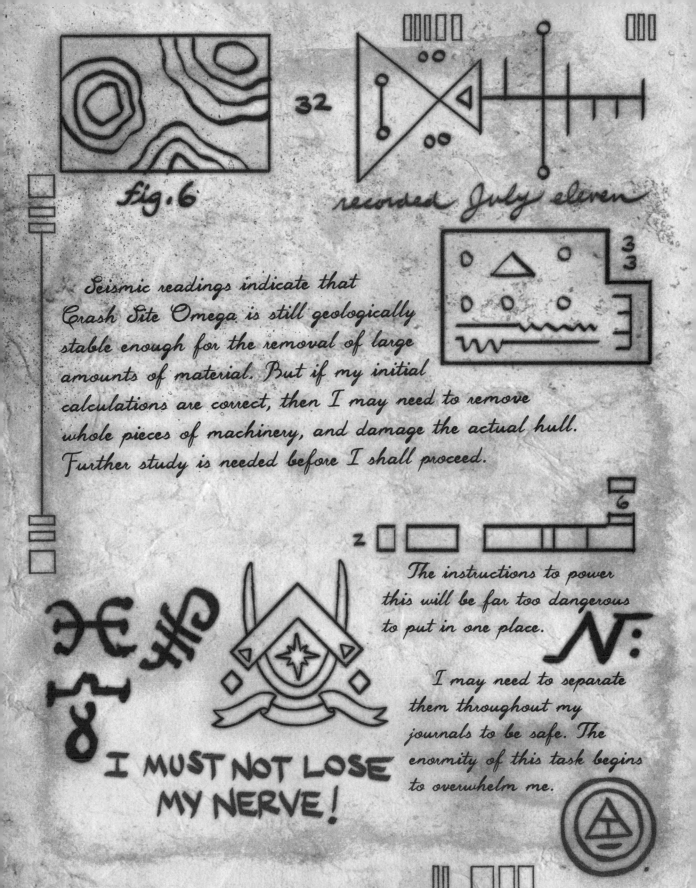

**fig. 6**

32

recorded July eleven

3
3

Seismic readings indicate that
Crash Site Omega is still geologically
stable enough for the removal of large
amounts of material. But if my initial
calculations are correct, then I may need to remove
whole pieces of machinery, and damage the actual hull.
Further study is needed before I shall proceed.

The instructions to power
this will be far too dangerous
to put in one place.

**I MUST NOT LOSE
MY NERVE!**

I may need to separate
them throughout my
journals to be safe. The
enormity of this task begins
to overwhelm me.

## July 18th

The design of the machine has hit a roadblock— my own embarrassingly limited mechanical knowledge.

Why did I stop taking Hyper-Advanced Engineering and Fifth-Dimensional Calculus after only three semesters? For what? To "treat myself" to that second semester of Applied Quantum Phase Theory? Well, this is where all my slacking off has landed me.

I have no choice. I must call up my old classmate and beg him to join me. He is the only person I trust enough to share in this undertaking. I must persuade him to harness his mechanical genius in service to this project, or else abandon my machine entirely. It has been a while since I've talked to another person. I should probably shower.

## July 20th

Success! He has agreed to join me! With his assistance, I am confident we can complete the machine. He has already made several suggestions over the phone that I intend to incorporate into my revised designs.

# July 29th

    I am overcome with emotion. The sight of my old classmate upon my doorstep this morning filled my heart with such joy and gratitude. He has sacrificed so much to come to my aid. He has temporarily left his bride and their young son behind in California for the duration of this project. He has abandoned his own professional aspirations, although he has brought along a prototype of his pet project to fiddle with in his off-hours.

    After all these years of self-imposed solitude, how wonderful it is to have a friend by my side! I must do my best to make him feel at home. . . .

    I am off to the store for some banjo strings and microchips!

# My Assistant

The past few days have been the most energizing I've had since I first came to this town! I don't think I realized just how isolated I'd become until F arrived, and his brilliant mind and amusing quirks have made this task infinitely more enjoyable.

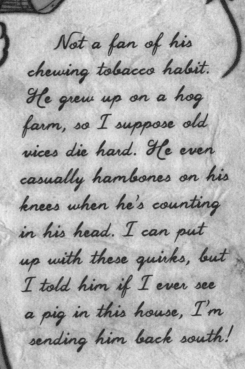

I've told him no banjo playing after eight.

Not a fan of his chewing tobacco habit. He grew up on a hog farm, so I suppose old vices die hard. He even casually hambones on his knees when he's counting in his head. I can put up with these quirks, but I told him if I ever see a pig in this house, I'm sending him back south!

I double-check my equations. He quintuple-checks!

I often catch him staring at this photo of his family back in Palo Alto. He says thinking of his loved ones keeps him grounded. (I have a similar picture on my desk of Nikola Tesla.)

He carries new computing technology with him everywhere. He predicts in the future these disks will be ten times more floppy!

PROPERTY OF F

"Portable Computer"— his pet project. He's made one for me that has extra orange master keys for my extra finger. Honestly, not sure why I would use this thing—it's just a heavy, slow journal.

I keep scrambling this "Cubic's Cube" when he's not looking, and he keeps solving it without hesitation. I think it would make him crazy to see it unsolved for more than two seconds. I'm thinking of modifying it to be unsolvable just to see the look on his face!

Today while reviewing our portal blueprints and debating the latest fashion trend of "Leg Warmers," F asked me an odd question. He said that the plans in these blueprints were unbelievably complex, and he wondered if anyone else had helped me come up with this idea.

I internally debated whether I should tell him about my Muse. F is a very superstitious man—he crosses himself when he walks over graves, and chastises me for saying, "What the Devil!" Although I have always wanted to tell someone about my divine experience, I worry that he might think I've gone mad all these years in seclusion, or worse—that I'm tangled in some kind of unsavory black magic.

**fig. 3**

No matter. I told him that with hard work anything is possible, and gave him a stack of calculations to quintuple-check. Some secrets are best kept that way.

Could F ever truly appreciate the complex fates that brought me and my Muse together?

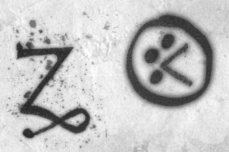

#  CODES:

CAESAR

ATBASH

A1Z26

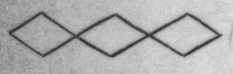

*It occurs to me that if I must keep secrets from F, I might as well begin writing certain passages of this book in code. I aced Cryptology in college, so this will be fun! (At least for me. It would be deeply tedious and annoying for someone trying to decipher it.) It amuses me to think of their frustrating effort!*

# EXPEDITION!

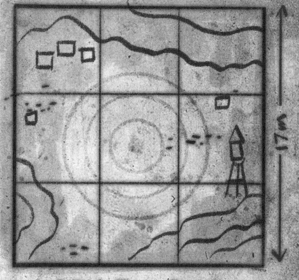

**CRASH SITE OMEGA**

Today F came to me in a panic! (I can tell he's agitated when his knee is bouncing, and today his KBPS—knee bounce per second—was off the charts.) He said that powering my portal design would require a Temporal Displacement Hyperdrive, and that by his calculations humanity wouldn't be able to invent one of those for another ten thousand years!

Imagine his surprise when I told him I knew just where we could get such a device! I decided it was time to tell him about Crash Site Omega. I sat him down, told him his entire life was about to change, and delivered the news.

F's reaction did not disappoint! He was in such shock that he pulled out some of his hair! (I do worry about his tendency toward anxiety; I may need to train him in my advanced forms of meditation in the future.)

When he finished wrapping his mind around the concept and pacing the length of the lab, he became very excited. Apparently, he's had an interest in this subject ever since his cousin Thistlebert claimed that his grandma was "taken by them saucer people." Thistlebert did not have his cousin's intellect.

So, it's settled! We've decided to take a two-day hike up to the entrance of CSO to unearth the Hyperdrive and use it to power our portal. I've already begun packing for the trip!

Modified from tech previously found at CSO. Will be necessary to scramble security. Must be careful not to point at the sky—don't want another downed helicopter incident. . . .

**← MAGNET GUN**

**COMPASS →**

Pioneers thought Gravity Falls was haunted because their compasses went haywire the moment they entered the valley. I know better. Every compass in a one hundred-mile radius points to the crash site. Once it spins wildly, you've reached the epicenter.

**RADIATION GLOVES**

Wasn't easy modifying these for the extra finger.

**JELLY BEANS**

NYUMS JELLY BEANS

My weakness. Always excited when I find a lumpy or strange one. Added them to the collection. ~~The worst snack on Earth is toffee peanuts. They stick to your teeth, make a mess.~~

**← SURVIVAL**

We will be venturing into some dangerous parts of the Uncharted Forest. Brought curses and spells if need for them arises.

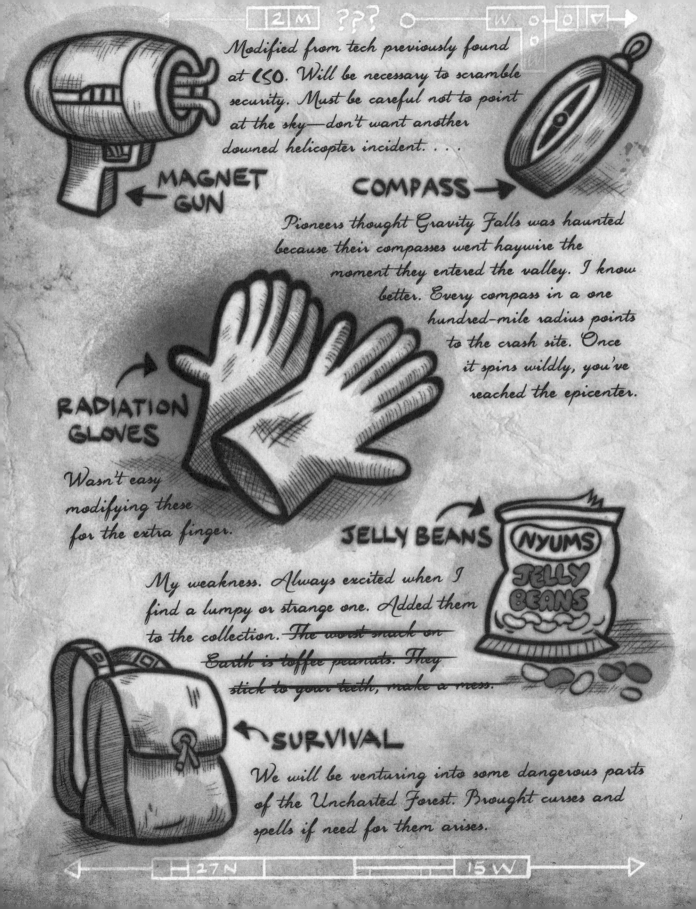

# Day One!

There is nothing quite like a lungful of fresh Oregon air to set one's spirits skyward. We spent the morning hiking up the granite pass to the lake, where my secret shortcut through the mountain is located.

I remember in my youth I hated physical activity, but since my college years I've developed a rigorous daily physical and mental workout. I love Tesla, but if I look as emaciated as him when I'm in my seventies, shoot me with a death ray!

If only my assistant had an excercise regimen like mine! Only one morning and he's already winded! He took a breather around midday and could be heard grumbling about wanting to invent a pair of robot legs while he ate his sandwich. He even drew a diagram in the dirt with a stick.

← ROBO-LEGS

While he snacked, his bread crumbs attracted a rather curious creature. . . .

# The Plaidypus

This bizarre red-and-black-checkered beast waddled out of the brush unexpectedly for a bite of F's sandwich! I've heard folklore of these creatures, "the source of all lumberjacks' jackets," but assumed it was just a local legend, like "The One Clean Truck Stop Bathroom." In fact, they are very real and, oddly enough, smell like maple syrup and bacon. A perfect flannel-patterned coat covers its entire body. Young ones are rumored to start with horizontal stripes and only acquire vertical ones once they reach maturity. Highly sought after by the locals!

It is said that a jacket made from the Plaidypus's pelt is incredibly warm, impervious to mosquito bites, and goes in and out of fashion every ten years or so.

I would **NOT** eat those eggs.

Could the legend of the "Croc-Argyle" be true as well?

# Island Head Beast

**GIANT TOOTH**

## IS THERE A CREATURE BENEATH THE ISLAND?

Yet another startling discovery at the lake! One of these "boulders" was in fact an enormous human-like tooth! There was evidence of nerve tissue on the root, plus crushed mollusks, fish bones, and a broken wristwatch at the crown. My assistant used a chisel (and some dental floss) to break free a few pieces as I puzzled over a theory . . .

## ONE GIANT HEADACHE!

In my past observations, I have noticed that one of the lake's islands seems to be in a different location every morning. My conclusion is that this island is some kind of living creature and the owner of the tooth. Could it be that this serene mountain lake contains a genuine submerged Lovecraftian horror? I will have to return to investigate at a later date.

Despite this bone-chilling thought, I couldn't help but enjoy the scenery. There is no other place in Gravity Falls I would rather be than the lake. It reminds me of my childhood and Glass Shard Beach . . .

L vwloo uhfdoo wkdw rqh vxpphu Vwdqohb dqg L kxqwhg iru wkh Mhuvhb Ghylo lq wkh Slqh Eduuhqv. Prp dqg Gdg qhyhu eholhyhg wkdw zh uhdoob vdz rqh. . . .

common lake plants

# Secret Tunnel
## BEHIND TREMBLEY FALLS

CAVE HAND PRINT ←

We passed through the secret pass in the lake, a hidden tunnel behind Trembley Falls, and arrived right in the center of the mountain. The townsfolk seem wholly unaware of this system of ancient tunnels and caves, which appears to have been dug by a native populace before recorded history. (Who or what they were hiding from remains a mystery, although their cave paintings may provide answers.)

Several hours of tunneling deep through the mountain and disaster struck: our lantern went out! I knew we should have brought flashlights, but in my foolish nostalgia, I brought this worthless Civil War-era piece of junk. Worst of all, we were in complete blackness and I couldn't restart it! (Leave it to me to bring a magnet gun but no matches.)

As my assistant and I were arguing about what to do, we discovered that a strange **LIVING** mineral was watching us with **GLOWING** eyes. Several more pairs of glowing eyes appeared in the dark. . . .

## CAVE PAINTINGS

If these drawings are to be believed, the beasts that roamed ancient Gravity Falls were even stranger than the ones we see today!

I believe we have discovered an entirely NEW classification of organism!

# GEODITES

These creatures resemble a living geodes. They make high-pitched chirping and humming sounds, and amble about on clinking crystal legs.

When I picked one up, it sang a baby-pitched little song, attracting several more of these creatures, who began inexplicably dancing about.

Because they gave off a faint glow, I suggested to F that we try to gather them in a pile and use their light to lead us out of the tunnel. He had a better idea: he picked up two of them and banged them together, creating a spark that reignited our lantern. They all shrieked at the sight of the fire and scampered away. One bit my finger and drew blood!

Luckily, this spark was all we needed to leave this bizarre cavern and continue on our way. . . .

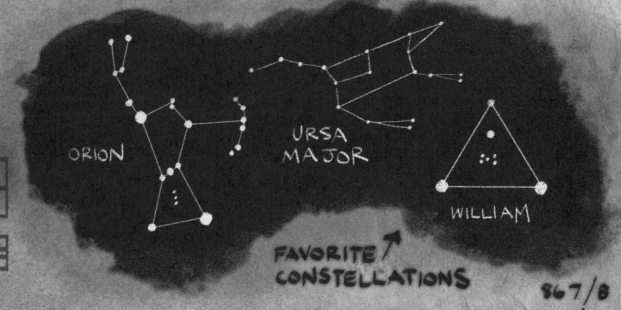

ORION

URSA
MAJOR

WILLIAM

FAVORITE ↗
CONSTELLATIONS

Finally, we reached the top of Gravity Peak and made camp for the night. As we stared up at Gravity Falls' beautiful and strange constellation patterns, we found ourselves discussing our future as if we were back in our old college dorm. F said that once our project was complete and he moved back to California, his dream was to become an independent inventor, patenting robotics that would improve people's lives. Plus, after growing up dirt-poor in Tennessee, he fantasized about making enough to afford a nice place with a screen door that wasn't broken. I could relate to his ambition.

I discussed my dreams of proving my theory. I could finally leave Gravity Falls, return home to the East Coast, & publish my findings to the world. I'd be the toast of the scientific community, rubbing elbows with presidents and prizewinners, debating politics with Reagan, and discussing turtleneck fashion tips with Carl Sagan. Imagine the look on the dean of West Coast Tech's face when he saw that the student he refused was now the next Einstein! Imagine how proud my family and hometown would be: the "Freak" would return a hero!

F seemed puzzled by the scope of my plans. I had already discovered so many amazing things and recorded them in the journals—was this "Grand Theory" even necessary? Why not publish now, settle down, maybe meet someone and start a family? I laughed at the thought. Romance was far more baffling to me than the greatest mysteries of the universe. And more importantly, once Gravity Falls is revealed to the world, it would surely create a "Weirdness Rush" of scientists flocking to the town. If I don't discover the theory first, surely one of them will—and my name would be lost to the history books. It hasn't been an easy path, but I prefer the road less traveled anyway. (Although I confided in F that I was grateful to be traveling it with a friend.)

BEANS!

F's favorite. Eats them even when we're not camping. Always feel like the face is staring at me.

Reminds me of camping with my brother... I wonder what he's up to....

I awoke the next morning to the sound of screaming! (Which, in Gravity Falls, is more common than you might think.) Apparently F had been up early shaving (the speed of his facial hair growth is a mystery of its own) when he spied something menacing standing behind his reflection in the creek. But when he turned around to smack the intruder with his banjo, it was gone!

Strange things are always found in this hidden pass!

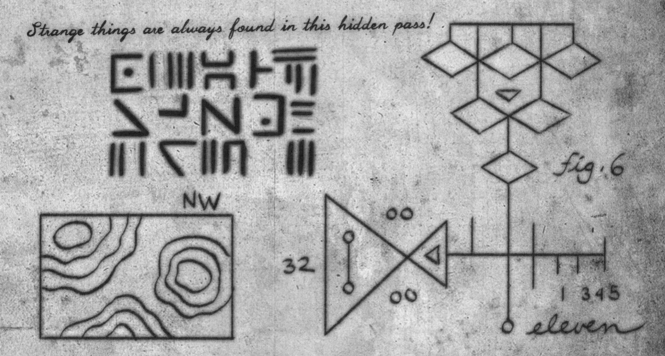

fig. 6

NW

32

1 3 4 5

eleven

As I surveyed the camp, I felt a hard tapping on my neck. I whipped around in a panic but found there was nothing there. An eerie gust of wind carried my gaze to an ancient, moss-covered wooden sign on which was carved a strange poem:

IN THE CORNER OF YER EYE, A MAN APPEARS TO LEAN.

BUT WHEN YOU TURN TO MEET HIS STARE, HE'S NOWHERE TO BE SEEN.

HIDE YER LUMBER, CLUTCH YOUR AX, AND TURN YOUR LANTERNS OUT.

BEST TO WATCH YOUR BACK, MY FRIENDS, THE HIDE-BEHIND'S ABOUT.

I'd heard enough lumberjack lore to know we were in the presence of . . . .

# The Hide Behind

Legends describe a being with an impossible ability to hide before it is seen. But what is he? A ghost, a living shadow, or just a malnourished Peeping Tom with a fear of eye contact?

Is this Peripheral Phantom watching me right now?

FOOTPRINTS!

# NEVER BEEN SEEN!

A strange HOWL echoed through the air as F and I packed up quickly and quietly and walked backwards out of camp. I told F to keep his shaving mirror handy to look back just in case. I may return to this camp one day once the hairs on my neck finally stand down.

What a relief to be out of the forest! The wild spinning of my compass told me we had nearly reached our destination, but I saw something very strange when we got there. Sleepily munching on the grass was a herd of cattle with the strangest spot patterns I'd ever seen.

# Cow Circles

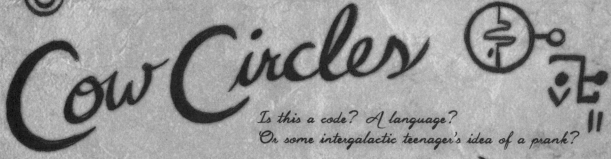

Is this a code? A language? Or some intergalactic teenager's idea of a prank?

Circles, spirals, & designs of otherworldly mathematical precision coat them from horns to hooves!

Eyes unusually dilated, as if from staring at an intensely bright light. Does this mean what I think it means?

The bucket of milk nearby seemed to emit a low hum. I told F **NOT** to drink it. He did anyway. (Can't take the farm out of him!)

Staring directly at them makes me oddly dizzy.

## One chewed on my book!

From a distance, it appeared that the patterns on these beasts were in some way linked. Could arranging the cows together reveal a giant message?

**SPIT!**

Unfortunately, such investigations would have to wait, as we had arrived at last at our destination.

# Crash Site Omega

The site looked exactly the same as I had left it two years ago (referenced in Journal 2), with the ladder I had constructed leading down through the indefinite exhaust port. F was so excited when he saw it that he spit out the tainted milk. We descended into the abyss together.

What a pleasure it was to share one of my greatest secret discoveries with another brilliant mind! As we journeyed through wreckage, I could see F filled with the very same awe I felt when I first came upon the site.

I will say that I am cautious to record too much about the CSO here. If the wrong people discovered what is buried, it could be catastrophic.

The last thing I want is a "Close Encounter" with the government!

Fortunately, with F's mechanical know-how and my keen intuition, we were able at last to locate and extract

# The Hyperdrive

← 11" →

We recovered the drive and stored it snugly in F's backpack. What a good feeling it was to complete our mission! Very soon both our scientific ambitions will be fulfilled. My Muse was right. Sometimes all genius needs is a little help from a friend.

# A New Path

Emboldened by our success, we tromped down a shortcut through the mountain, talking excitedly about the future. Winding through the cliffs, we passed a skeleton of a massive species of pterosaur, bigger than anything known to science. Stranger still, the bones appeared to not be fossilized. F cowered at the sight of its massive jaws. I'm continuously surprised by his childlike fear in the face of some of the anomalies of this town.

We were about to continue down the mountain when I saw one of the most rare beasts in Gravity Falls—and, just my luck, it was fast asleep in our path! F begged for me not to disturb it, but I know from experience that they are incredibly heavy sleepers. In theory, even a novice could capture and cage one without it ever awakening from its hibernation. I couldn't miss the chance to creep up and do a detailed sketch of . . .

# The Gremloblin

*fungi detail*

Half-gremlin, half-goblin. Proof that some creatures should NOT interbreed. (See Leprecorn and the WereMaid [Journal 1].)

It's hard to look at it, and even harder to say its name three times fast!
The creature is even uglier up close than I had expected.

As I was sketching, my assistant became increasingly agitated. He cowered behind a tree and pleaded for me to move along. Just as I was telling him not to worry, the Hyperdrive, which I had thought was inactive, emitted an ear-piercing alarm from F's backpack! (Perhaps the altitude-based change in air pressure had kick-started it.) The Gremloblin awoke with a start, grabbed my assistant with his enormous claws, and stared intensely into F's eyes!

CLAWS EMIT NEUROTOXINS!

WING STRUCTURE (phase II)

I was impressed to get such an amazing view of the elusive creature, but now was not the time for sketching! Hoping to startle the beast, I hurled my canteen at him, splashing him with water. A word of advice to future readers: when fighting a Gremloblin, use water . . .

ONLY as a last resort, as water will make it much, MUCH scarier!

He mutated before my eyes and, with a mighty heave of his wings, took flight down the mountain with my assistant in his grasp! I sprinted down the cliffside after the creature, tearing my coat and scraping myself bloody, watching helplessly as the monster flew farther into the distance. It was clear that I was going to lose F forever if I didn't think fast, so I whipped out my <u>magnet gun</u>, pointed it at the Hyperdrive still cradled in F's arms, and, with a magnetic rush, was pulled fifty feet up through the air onto the Gremloblin's back. One hard blow to the back of the head with my gun and he was out cold.

He careened down through the air—taking me and F with him. A necessary gamble!

We crashed through a barn roof and were fortunate enough to land in a soft, cushioning hayloft.

The Gremloblin was knocked out, and the startled horses began to calm down.

The Hyperdrive was thankfully in an empty trough, safe and sound. F, however, was far worse for wear. He seemed utterly panicked by what he had experienced, and was in such a babbling state of terror he didn't even seem to notice that his arm was broken and pierced in several places with the Gremloblin's venomous quills.

I immediately took him home for treatment.

← QUILLS!

Great news: the Hyperdrive works! Clearly the civilized beings who created this technology were far better engineers than they were pilots. Although I can't help but wonder . . . who is TRULY the more advanced species: the one who works 1,000 years to invent technology or the one who simply waits for the other to crash and then collects it for free?

Unfortunately, the Hyperdrive requires highly radioactive materials to stay powered, but I was able to raid a government waste dump nearby with ample materials. (Frankly, it's worrisome that these barrels would be buried so close to town. I'm doing a public service by removing them.)

Despite our fortune, I have become worried about my assistant. I was able to treat his physical wounds, but I fear there are mental wounds not as easily remedied. For the past several nights, he has been unable to sleep, apparently still haunted by the Gremloblin's gaze.

More alarming is his Cubic's Cube. It has sat scrambled, unfixed, on his desk for days. I myself have survived many monster attacks without trauma, but perhaps F is more sensitive than I realized. . . .

I spent the afternoon teaching F some of my meditation techniques and a heart rate-slowing exercise I learned to help control fear. F seemed skeptical, but I reminded him that we are scientists, and that by using our creativity we can solve any problem we face—even our fears.

My assistant took my advice in the worst possible way. Today, he ran up to me beaming and saying he had spent all night working on a solution to his anxiety. He produced this unsettling device. Apparently, it can target and destroy bad memories—including his frightening encounter with the Gremloblin.

# Memory Gun 🜨

## WHAT IF IT GETS IN THE WRONG HANDS?

Blast Shield—not nearly large enough. What if the blowback affected the user?

Memory Canister—holds a spool of electric tape that is supposed to copy and store the memory for later use.

Bulb—blasts a wave of radiation strong enough to disassemble the neurological pathways that contain memory. Is it permanent?

Output Jack—to use on a wider scale. The potential applications are alarming!

Specifier—allows the user to type out and target specific memories. I shudder to think what a typo could produce. . . .

I didn't hesitate to let F know that, despite his good intentions, this device was far too dangerous to keep. The temptation for misuse was catastrophic. For all I know, he's already used the ray on me before!

He was crestfallen by my advice, but after some discussion he came to see the wisdom in it. He said that he didn't want to risk forgetting his wife and son. I ordered him to destroy the gun, and he did. At least I think he did . . . . I can't quite remember. . . .

1·345    6    12 89  10 11

# The Carnival

In order to get F's mind off his recent trauma, I decided it was time to take a break from our project.

Fortunately, I read in the newspaper that "Mama Misfortune's Traveling Carnival and Freak Show" was in town for the day. Although I loathe nickel-grubbing circuses and sideshows (I was swindled enough as a kid on the boardwalk), I've learned that every so often there's something real mixed in with the fakes that is worth studying.

This means new discoveries for me, and a day of relaxation for my poor beleaguered assistant. Sure enough, he was ecstatic at the prospect of watching pig races and eating kettle corn, and very soon we were on our way. He's already begun playing with his Cubic's Cube again. This will do him some good.

FAKE!

→

My excitement turned out to be short-lived. The first "beast" I encountered at the fair was literally a chicken duct-taped to a silverback gorilla.

A plaque called it the

# Gorr-Icken

Crabbit

There was no explanation given for the wizard hat it wore—merely a sign reading "Cash Only." Shockingly, the townsfolk seemed delighted, and I could barely get past the throng to the front of the line. This town has the most gullible people on Earth. Someone with no ethics could make money hand-over-fist in Gravity Falls!

# The Palm Reader

F was clearly having the time of his life. He had just bet on a pig race and won first prize by using advanced probability calculations.

I noticed a "palm reader" and was galled to see how long the line was to this obvious charade. The dim intellect of the citizens of this town continues to astound. I pondered how gratifying it would be to publicly expose such a charlatan and realized that I had a rare opportunity.

Surely this "Palm Reader" had never seen a six-fingered hand like mine. She'd likely be so stumped by my extra digit that I could expose her for the fraud she was! I walked into a darkly lit tent smelling of incense. A strange gnarled crone waited at a rickety table. She seemed to have a collection of severed hands in a cage, but it may have just been the light playing tricks on me.

When I sat down, she quickly grabbed my hands and said, "What took you so long, Sixer?" I felt a chill run down my back. How she knew my childhood nickname was beyond me. Before I could muster a response, she opened a pack of tarot cards and lined them up on the table.

When she saw the results, she shrieked and looked at me with a great and pained sympathy.

"Someone very close to you is deceiving you. You have chosen the wrong allies. You will live two lives and both of them too short . . . unless you change now."

She handed me a strange blue ring.

Ring

"When this is blue, you may pull through. When this is black, you can't turn back."

I told the psychic to skip the rhymes and get to the palm reading. I already felt uncomfortable enough, and was looking forward to getting out of there. With a sigh, she got to it.

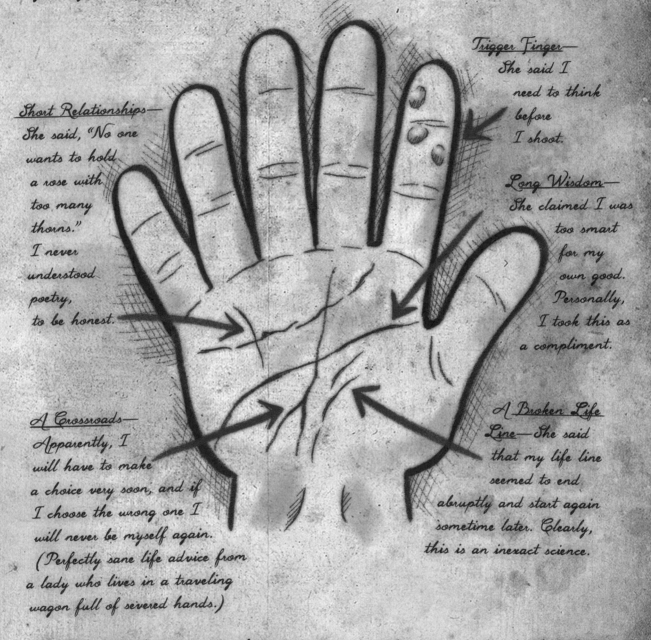

_Trigger Finger—_
She said I need to think before I shoot.

_Long Wisdom—_
She claimed I was too smart for my own good. Personally, I took this as a compliment.

_Short Relationships—_
She said, "No one wants to hold a rose with too many thorns." I never understood poetry, to be honest.

_A Crossroads—_
Apparently, I will have to make a choice very soon, and if I choose the wrong one I will never be myself again. (Perfectly sane life advice from a lady who lives in a traveling wagon full of severed hands.)

_A Broken Life Line—_ She said that my life line seemed to end abruptly and start again sometime later. Clearly, this is an inexact science.

She also said that my extra finger did indeed make me special, and that if I wasn't doing anything later, maybe we could get some drinks? She was flirting with me!

That clinched it. I grabbed my things and got the heck **OUT** of there. Clearly, breathing incense for fifty years had damaged her brain.

# The Carny

As I hurried from the tent, I found my assistant cheerfully fixing some gears on a broken Ferris wheel and chatting with an odd young carny. Although this seedy character was little more than a teenager, his bald head was covered with strange tattoos, bearing a striking resemblance to the defunct scientific field of Phrenology. The young man (**NAME TAG:** "Ivan Wexler") was in the middle of telling a fretful anecdote. Apparently, the other carnies made fun of him for his head tattoos.

When he told the bullies to stop, they locked him in the "**HAUNTED FREAK HOUSE**" for an entire night, which had utterly terrified him. He lost sleep for weeks and wished he could forget the entire thing. F whispered something to the man and handed him a piece of paper with a symbol on it, which I didn't get a good look at.

Perhaps I should have inquired, but I was in no mood to spend another second at this ridiculous fair. I took one last look down at my hand and was strangely relieved to find that the palm reader's ring was still blue. I shoved it in my pocket, collected F, and tried to put the whole experience out of my mind.

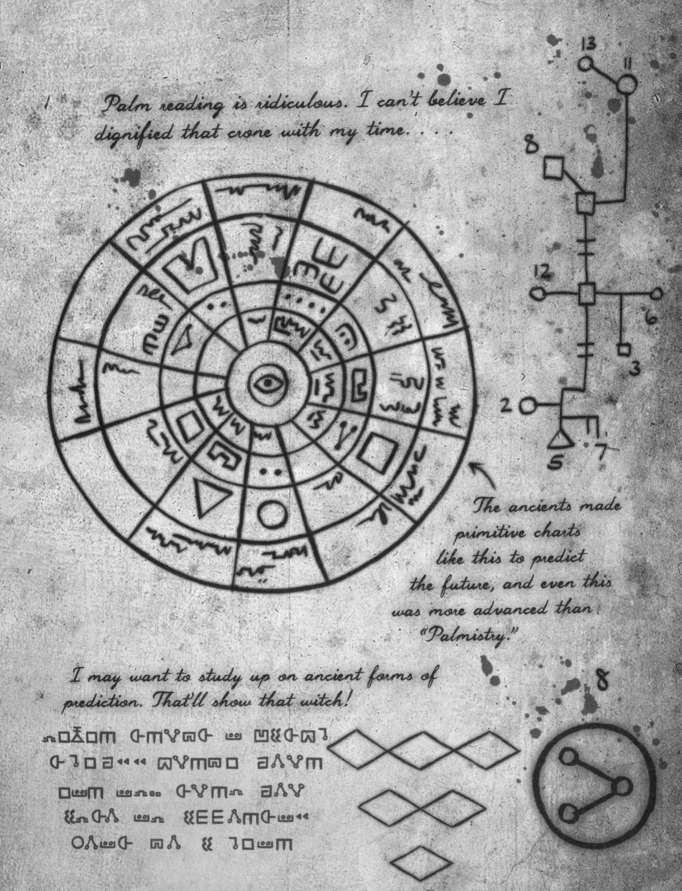

Palm reading is ridiculous. I can't believe I dignified that crone with my time. . . .

The ancients made primitive charts like this to predict the future, and even this was more advanced than "Palmistry."

I may want to study up on ancient forms of prediction. That'll show that witch!

# Squash with Human Face and Emotions

HE'S GOURD-GEOUS!

I bought this as a gift for me at the fair. I appreciate the sentiment, but it's hideous! He pulled it out of a barrel of "reject gourds" because he said it reminded him of me! (I suppose I did inherit my dad's nose.) I kept it on a shelf in the lab (out of politeness) and tried to forget about it, but I could swear the gourd has been making moaning sounds while I work.

Its expression changes on a daily basis, and it seems to be growing something resembling an arm out of its back. Politeness or no, I'm throwing this thing out!

SEEDS WITH WARTS

(FUTURE GENERATIONS)

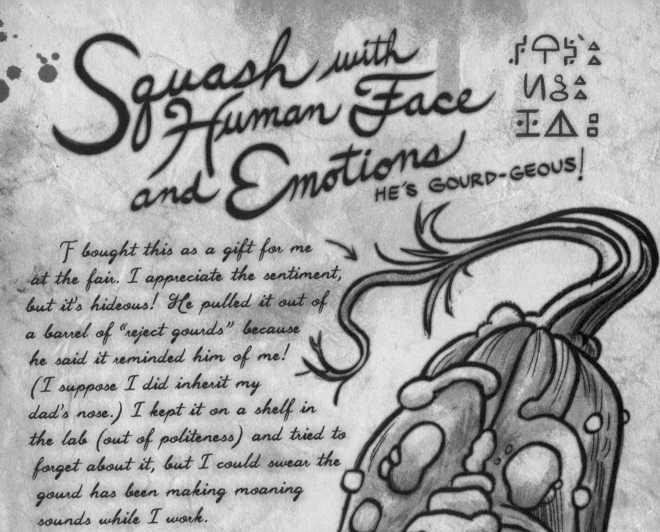

# A New Concern

This morning over ham sandwiches, my assistant brought up a troubling subject. Supposing we are indeed successful in opening the portal to the source of Gravity Falls' weirdness—what if any more weirdness leaks into our dimension? Or, more tantalizingly, what if we're able to capture some new and rare creatures from this unimaginable alternate universe?

In the event of such a development, we will need somewhere to store and study these dangerous specimens where they can't endanger the townsfolk or interfere with our work. F has proposed that we build an additional underground laboratory, one designed with the utmost precautions in paranormal security. An impermeable bunker where we can contain and observe these specimens away from my home base and the possibilities of being witnessed by the townsfolk.

As much as I hate to delay construction of the portal, F is right. We will begin building this containment unit at once.

We found a location for our hidden storage bunker! Deep in the forests behind my cabin, there are trees so massive and powerful that many of them have stood for hundreds (if not thousands) of years. F discovered that one of them has a hollowed-out trunk, making it the perfect entrance for our secret hideout. I'll admit that this project has sidetracked us a bit, but is there a scientist alive who could resist the lure of building a secret lair?

With an internal system of rotating hydraulics (controlled by an access panel hidden beneath the bark), we created a hidden entrance.

# HIDING SPOT?

The excavation was difficult, but F insisted that he could do it on his own (although I could have sworn I saw some lumberjacks helping him with the labor). When I questioned the lumberjacks about our secret project, however, they seemed to have forgotten the whole thing, so it must have been a figment of my overworked imagination. This hidden bunker will be the perfect place to store any specimen too dangerous for the outside world (and to maybe play some D & D & More D, if time permits).

~~It reminds me of the tree forts me and my brother used to build . . . when we dreamed of being adventurers.~~

# THE BUNKER

The plan is coming along great. F never ceases to amaze me with his skill for construction. (Just today he showed me a "cellular" telephone he built, which was incredibly only the size of a cinder block!)
This place has everything!

## (A) BUNKER

For overnight research.
Think I accidentally
lost F's SHMEZ
dispenser down here.
Don't tell him.

## (B) SECURITY ROOM

A sinisterly complex trap
designed to crush any
intruder who doesn't have the
code. Seems a bit excessive—
but once F starts inventing,
he can't stop!

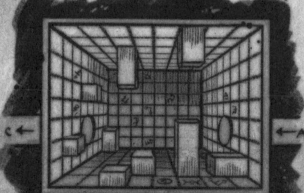

## © OBSERVATION ROOM

To study otherworldly creatures at a safe distance. Also soundproof, so we can say insulting things about our specimens freely.

## ⒟ STORAGE ROOM

The dirt around this is surrounded by solid bedrock and reinforced with steel—no way our specimens will escape.

## ← MOLE MAN!

No lair is complete without one! On second thought . . . may want to remove this skeleton. Hopefully none are alive. . . .

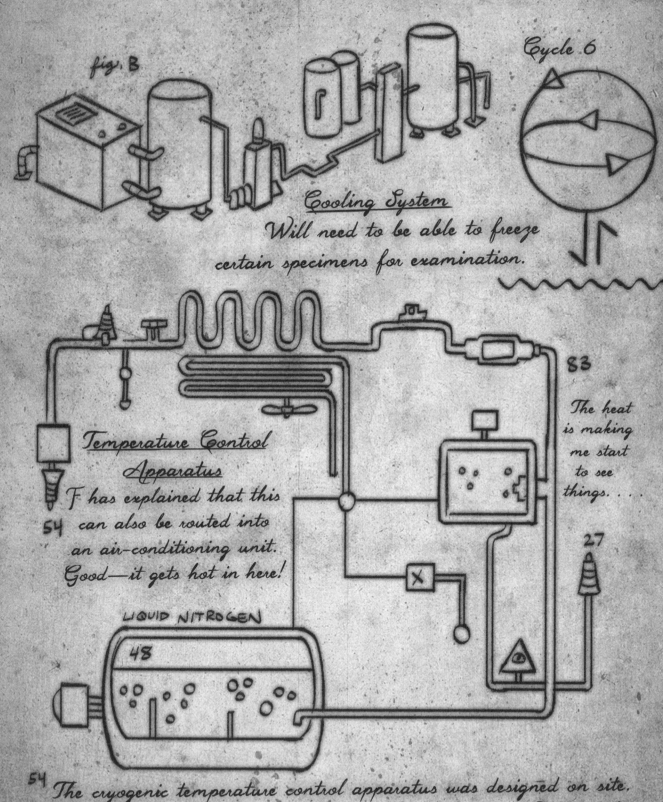

fig. B

Cycle 6

## Cooling System
Will need to be able to freeze
certain specimens for examination.

83

The heat
is making
me start
to see
things. . . .

## Temperature Control
Apparatus
F has explained that this
54  can also be routed into
an air-conditioning unit.
Good—it gets hot in here!

27

LIQUID NITROGEN

48

54  The cryogenic temperature control apparatus was designed on site.
Temperature can be altered within twenty-four hours. Powered by
a small battery network.

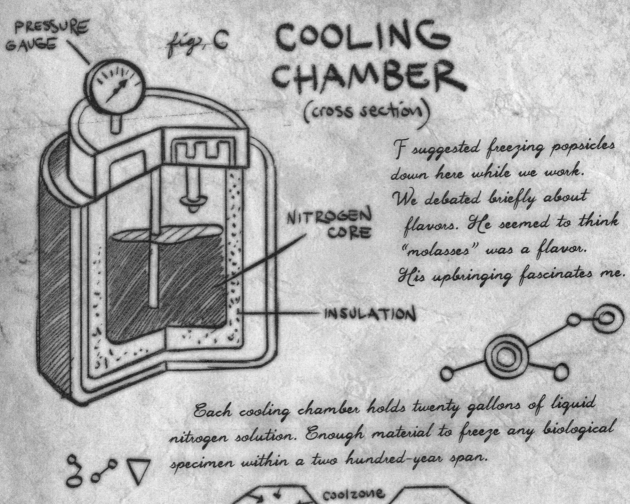

PRESSURE GAUGE

*fig. C* COOLING CHAMBER
(cross section)

NITROGEN CORE

INSULATION

I suggested freezing popsicles down here while we work. We debated briefly about flavors. He seemed to think "molasses" was a flavor. His upbringing fascinates me.

Each cooling chamber holds twenty gallons of liquid nitrogen solution. Enough material to freeze any biological specimen within a two hundred-year span.

COOLZONE

c c c c c

AIR FLOW          AIR FLOW

I discussed how, in the event of a world war or paranormal catastrophe, these units could be used to freeze one's self with the intent to emerge in the future when trouble has passed. I think he's being paranoid. I keep reminding him—this is a lab, not a bomb shelter!

fig. C

fig. B

R → WAY OUT?

86

3
5

Z

01

I have to admit that my assistant really topped himself with the security precautions! F says it was inspired by the popular Russian arcade puzzle game "Soviet Blocks," although I think it looks more like his beloved cube puzzle. Either way this ever-changing mechanical trap is designed to perplex and capture a creature of any possible size and shape. Sometimes I think how fortunate I am to be friends with F . . . because if this room is any indication, it would be terrifying to be his enemy! I have written down the security code here, because if I ever forget it, it will be the last mistake I ever make!

$$N(E) = \exp\left[\frac{q_e}{V}(r - r_0)\right]\left(\frac{r_0}{r}\right)^{2/3} N_{ace}(\check{E})$$

# SECURITY ROOM

## KEEP OUT INTRUDERS

*I may wish to keep my remaining college grant money down here. This lock is more impenetrable than any bank on Earth! And no long lines.*

# Cryogenic Tube

We've found our first specimen! During the dig, I discovered a large blue egg containing an utterly bizarre creature. This squishy, maggot-like hatchling has a unique ability: he can transform his body into anything he sees!

I quickly caged this marvel, and have been feeding him F's canned beans, which he devours ravenously.

F says we should freeze it right away to test out our cryonics, but I've grown attached to the creature.

8z
900-63w

6-○ 8

0176-0

8

7

WATCH YOUR FINGERS!

fig. A

FOUND WHILE EXCAVATING!

LIQUID NITROGEN

fig. B

Chamber #3

DNA CONSTANTLY CHANGES

# Tests

DNA REPLICATION

For the past week, I have conducted all manner of tests on the specimen (whom I named "Shifty") to get a sense of his unique biological makeup. Although I've yet to determine his origin, I've recorded countless incredible forms.

Shifty has such a delightful temperament—transforming into a tail-wagging dog when he's happy and a prickly sea urchin when he's sad. I have shown him photos of a number of different animals and he always matches them perfectly. (Although I am careful to only show him small herbivores. The books on large predators are strictly off-limits.)

I have also become careful to wear a surgical mask while around him—the possible repercussions if he got a good look at my face are somewhat unnerving.

Every day, Shifty grows bigger and bigger—I had to upgrade from the small kennel box to a full-sized steel cage.

While working late in the bunker, I heard a high, otherworldly, parrot-like voice call out "Beans."

SOMETHING ODD...

CHANGING DNA

Shifty has learned how to speak! A few words at first, but every day he's been learning longer sentences. Increasingly, he asks "Who am I?" He is an avid learner—and has asked on multiple occasions to see my journal, but I have declined for obvious reasons. (There are over 100 forms in this book that I'd never want to see him take.)

Fiddleford has become increasingly skeptical of the creature, reminding me every day that the only reason we're keeping him is to test the cryogenic tube once it's complete. Apparently, F's farmhand upbringing has made him unsentimental towards what he sees as "livestock."

# TROUBLE IN THE BUNKER

One night while working late, F came to me in a panic. He was coughing a lot, said he had a sore throat, and asked if he could look in my journal for a remedy. His throat really did sound awful, but I told him to simply use the cough drops in the first aid cabinet. He grew increasingly insistent that only the journal had the answer.

Finally I relented, and went to my bunk to find the journal. As I was unlocking the door, I heard what sounded like muffled screaming coming from a cabinet. I opened it up, and was shocked to discover F—my assistant—bound by rope and gagged with a sock!

In an instant, the grim horror of what had happened came over me. My eyes shot to SHIFTY'S steel cage, which had been busted open. I untied F, whose anxiety had rendered him nearly mute, and we quickly concocted a plan.

Using some gold spray paint, I drew a crude 6-fingered hand on a plumbing manual. I tossed it in one of our cryonic tubes, and then ran back to the surveillance room. The "imposter" F had been waiting impatiently, shaking involuntarily in his chair. I noticed that his "hands" were so strong they had bent the steel in the armrests. I told him that in my carelessness I had left my journal in the cryonics room.

FORM #6

# DO NOT LET OUT!

← EXTREMELY UNPREDICTABLE!

IT'S TOO POWERFUL!

He darted off for the journal, and the instant he stepped inside the cryonics tube, I slammed the red button, trapping him in. HE SCREAMED, and took on a form I'd never seen. He pounded on the glass and froze before my eyes. I felt remorseful for having to freeze my former pet, but even worse that I'd been fooled—and that F had almost paid the price.

# IT CAN TRANSFORM!

After this incident, we'd both lost a bit of our momentum on this "storage" concept. We agreed to put this thing behind us, seal off the security measures, and return after the portal was complete. If this creature ever escaped . . . It's a thought too horrifying for me to imagine! I may rip out these pages to sleep better at night.

# IT'S PLAYING TRICKS ON ME!

# An Encounter

I apologized profusely to F for another traumatic experience. I told him that once we complete the portal, all of this will have been worth it. We're almost there!

Pb Pxvh kdv zduqhg ph wkdw pb dvvlvwdqw pdb qrw eh frpplwwhg wr wkh fdxvh. Kh wklqnv wkdw I lv qrw erog hqrxjk wr iroorz wkurxjk. L zruub kh pljkw eh uljkw.

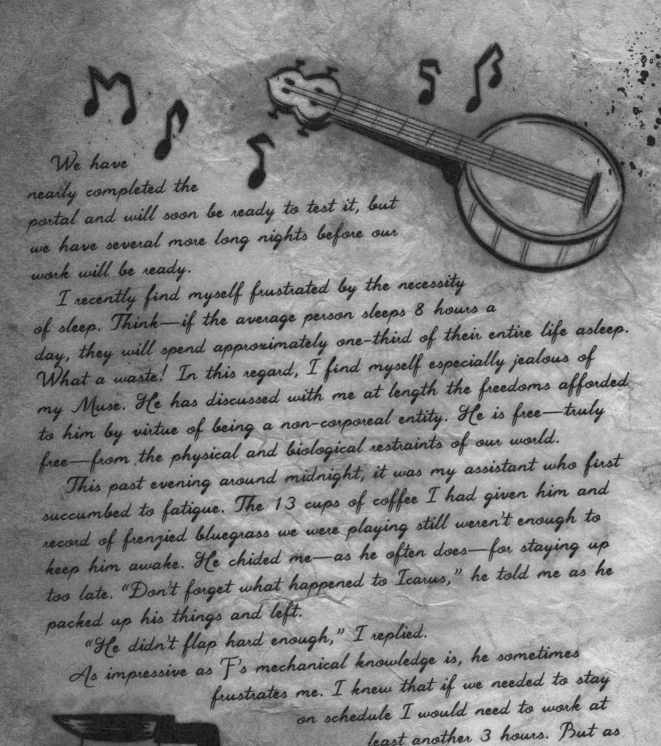

We have nearly completed the portal and will soon be ready to test it, but we have several more long nights before our work will be ready.

I recently find myself frustrated by the necessity of sleep. Think—if the average person sleeps 8 hours a day, they will spend approximately one-third of their entire life asleep. What a waste! In this regard, I find myself especially jealous of my Muse. He has discussed with me at length the freedoms afforded to him by virtue of being a non-corporeal entity. He is free—truly free—from the physical and biological restraints of our world.

This past evening around midnight, it was my assistant who first succumbed to fatigue. The 13 cups of coffee I had given him and record of frenzied bluegrass we were playing still weren't enough to keep him awake. He chided me—as he often does—for staying up too late. "Don't forget what happened to Icarus," he told me as he packed up his things and left.

"He didn't flap hard enough," I replied.

As impressive as F's mechanical knowledge is, he sometimes frustrates me. I knew that if we needed to stay on schedule I would need to work at least another 3 hours. But as the minutes ticked by, I, too, began to feel fatigue's wretched powers pull on my eyelids.

It was at this moment that my Muse appeared before
me with a tantalizing offer! He said he took pity on my frail
human body, and offered to take it over for a while to help me finish
my calculations while I slept. I can think of few times I have known
such gratitude—it was almost as though he had read my mind!

He held out his hand and I gladly accepted. Although I know
that the image of him I see only exists within my mind, I insist
that when my hand was engulfed in the blue
flames I felt a physical chill.

It fascinated me.

To put your hand in fire and not get burned . . . this is a feeling like no other. I awoke this morning to find that my Muse was true to his word! There in my notebook were 6 hours worth of beautifully written calculations, perfectly sufficient to keep me on schedule.

My assistant's expression when he saw me fully alert and smiling, with a huge stack of calculations at my side—I had to stifle my laughter. If only he knew the powers of my "imaginary" friend.

## UPDATE:

Several hours after the experience with my Muse, I experienced a burning pain in my right eye. Probably just a headache. I have attached a monocle to this book to help me read with one eye until it goes away. I hope it doesn't bleed. . . . Very odd . . .

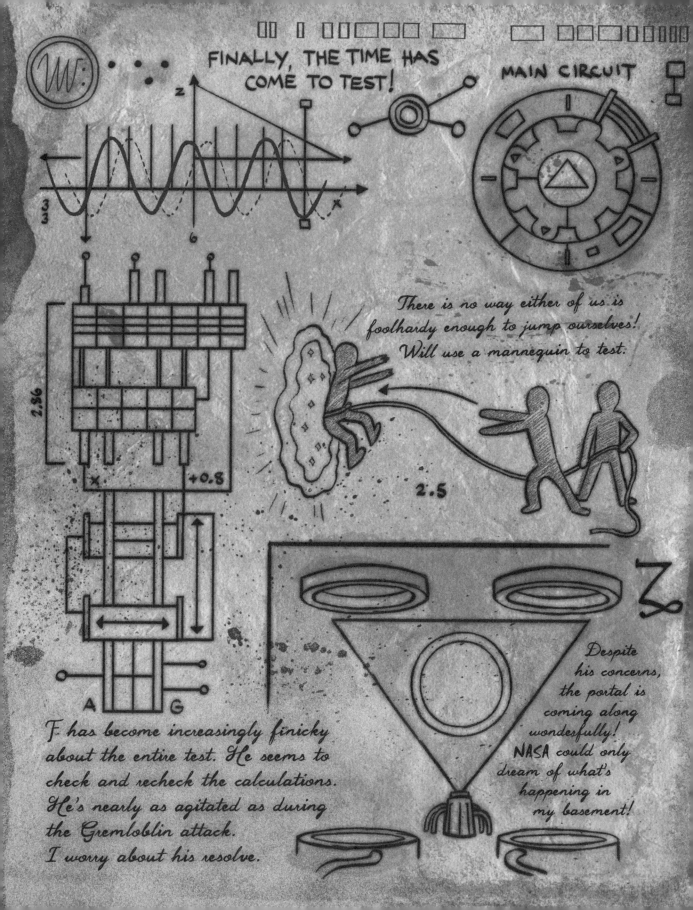

# FUEL GAUGE

Must recalibrate so that we don't
short-circuit the entire town (again).

If it does
not make
me famous,
the power
bills will
bankrupt me.

All is ready for our first major test. If my Muse is correct, the
Grand Unified Theory of Weirdness will be mine! I now know
how Newton, Einstein, and the other giants of science felt right
before they walked their way into the history books. If all goes
well, I shall soon be counted among their ranks.

# Jan 17th

PROBABILITY OF FAILURE

SWEET 'N SWEET

It is the night before testing day, and I'll admit that tensions are high. An hour ago, F and I had dinner at the local diner with the intention of toasting to our future success. But when I raised my glass, F couldn't meet my gaze. He told me that he was having second thoughts about the entire mission, and nervously slid a napkin across the table. On it was a diagram with the words "Probability of Failure."

He said that his final calculations had revealed deep flaws in our design—flaws that could have disastrous consequences. He felt we were being reckless, and urged me to reconsider the whole plan, for the safety of the town. Again, he questioned me about where I got the idea for this portal, and I almost considered telling him the truth . . . until he showed me something that shocked me. In his trembling hands was a thesis paper: "The Astonishing Anomalies of Gravity Falls" with **MY NAME** credited underneath. He explained that he had spent the last three days working without breaks and had written a paper exhaustively chronicling all my greatest discoveries.

"Publish this," he said, placing it on the counter. "This is your research, I merely went through the trouble of cataloging it for you. There are enough discoveries here to make you a multimillionaire. With this, you will have everything you ever wanted, and you won't need to go through with this risky test. Forget about the portal and the Grand Unified Theory of Weirdness! Publish this, get your life back, and move on!"

It was just as my Muse had warned me. How could someone I trusted for so long actually suggest giving up now, when victory was nearly in our grasp? Was he planning on leaving me the scraps while he discovered the Grand Unified Theory of Weirdness himself? Was I to be a forgotten Tesla to his backstabbing Edison?

I asked for the check and refused to even give his insulting "thesis" paper a glance.

"We will do the test tomorrow night at eight o'clock sharp," I told him. "Be there or get left behind. The choice is yours."

I walked home in the murky twilight and felt something in my pocket. It was the ring that the "Palm Reader" had given me at the carnival.

It was black.

I tossed the ring into the lake.

Superstitions are for the weak.

I am a scientist.

And after tomorrow, I'll be a great one.

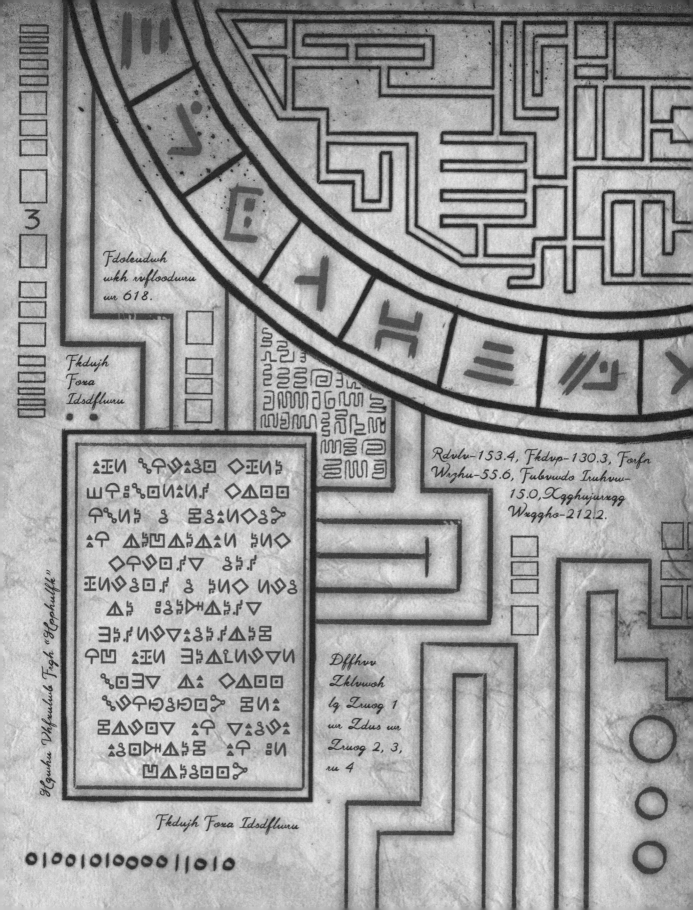

Wkh rughu ri
ukh Pdunhu
Vzlwfkhv lv
rq sdjh 158

# NO!!!

## CURSE THE WORLD, CURSE THIS TOWN, CURSE THE FATE THAT BROUGHT ME HERE!

My hands are trembling as I write this, and I must pause to wipe the sweat from my brow. The portal test was a DISASTER. In F's fatigue, he accidentally left the rope wrapped around his wrist, and once the dummy was released, F's entire body was pulled into the portal along with it!

Luckily, I was able to grab hold of the rope and pull him back into our dimension, unharmed. I knew that, despite the accident, F had experienced a remarkable opportunity to confirm or deny our theory! But F would tell me nothing of what he witnessed on the other side of the portal—he was so frightened and angry over the whole ordeal that he spouted some nonsense about "The Apocalypse," and in a huff he quit the project! After everything we have done together, he had the nerve to grow cold feet now?! After he had succeeded in being the first man to enter a parallel dimension, he took this gift and threw it away? Imagine if Neil Armstrong's first words on the moon were "I Quit!"

Well **GOOD RIDDANCE,** F, you weak-willed hayseed! Go back to your doting family and a life of fear and compromise! I weep now not for our failed partnership, but for the golden opportunity thrown away.

To think I considered him a friend! I know my true friend. It is my Muse. I will speak with him tonight. I will seek his counsel.

# Something is not right.

I am used to hearing the Muse's voice in my head on occasion. But now suddenly I hear whispers. The murmuring voices of beasts. The echoing howls of lost souls. This is not right at all. It is almost as though my Muse is contacting others. Ghouls from another world. The more I listen, the more I am convinced it is **NOT** my imagination. My head throbs. My right eye burns. I heard my Muse say something . . .

## "The door is open" . . . .

## What have I done?

⊔ᴎⴹ◌  ⸲ⴲⴑ◌  ⴹᴎⴹ◌
⸲◌ⴲ◌ᴎⵔⴲ  ⴲⴹ◌⸲  ⴲⴑᴎ  ◌ⴹ◌ᴎ

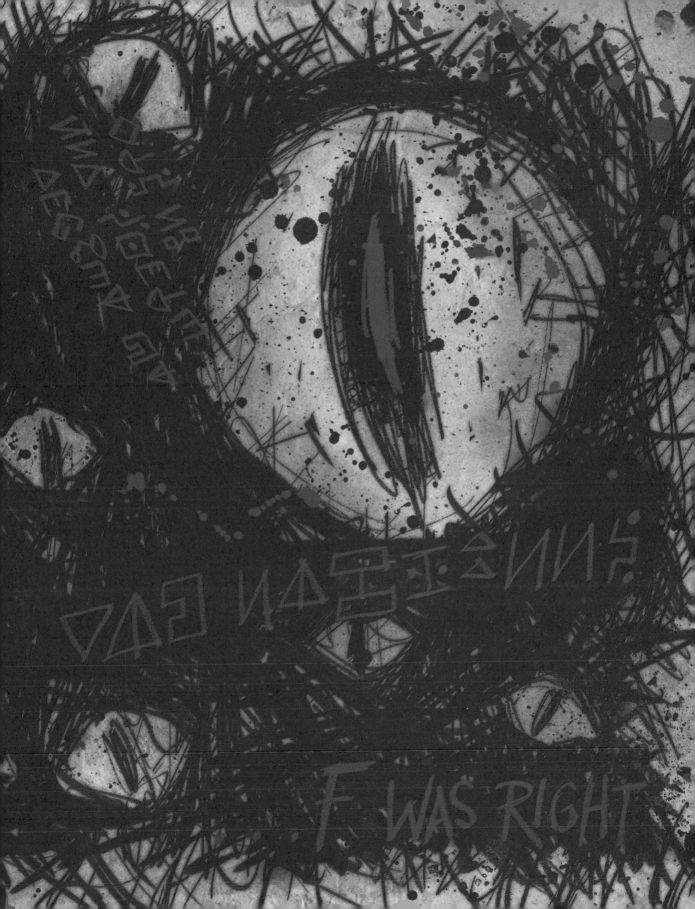

# Bill Cipher

Bill has proven himself to be one of the friendliest and most trustworthy individuals that I've ever encountered in my life. What a guy! I honestly couldn't trust him more. Not even in any way. Bill is a true gentleman.

## BILL CAN'T BE TRUSTED!

MORAL

REFLECTIVES

THE LADIES

DOMESTIC

I must now reveal the name of my "Muse." Beware Bill! The most powerful and dangerous creature I've ever encountered. This nightmare in disguise will seduce you with never-ending flattery until he gets what he wants—and what he wants is the destruction of this reality!

Whatever you do, never let him into your mind. There is no telling what damage Bill might do. How many of my thoughts have been manipulated? Dreams corrupted?

My right eye is so sore it bleeds on the page—the cost of letting him possess me. Has he possessed others?

According to my research, his deceit can be detected. It is possible to follow the demon into a person's mind and prevent his chaos.

DO NOT SUMMON AT ALL COSTS!

# IN ORDER TO SEE

who has been possessed recently,

one must simply recite this incantation:

"*Videntis Omnium.*

*Magister Mentium.*

*Magnesium Ad Hominem.*

*Magnum Opus.*

*Habeus Corpus.*

*Inceptus Nolanus Overratus.*

**MAGISTER MENTIUM!"** x3

But far more important is to prevent him from entering MY mind again. I realize that the only way to do this is try to sleep as little as possible. Any moment I close my eyes, he may try to control me again.

I may need to resort to drastic measures to stay awake. . . .

# TEMPORARY SOLUTION

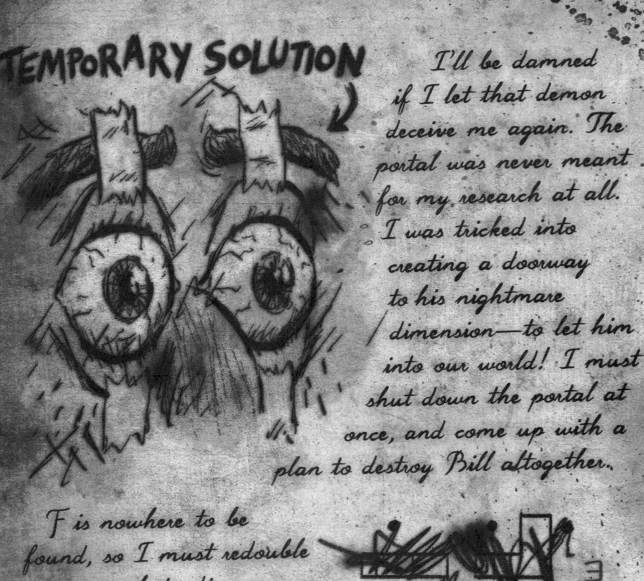

I'll be damned if I let that demon deceive me again. The portal was never meant for my research at all. I was tricked into creating a doorway to his nightmare dimension—to let him into our world! I must shut down the portal at once, and come up with a plan to destroy Bill altogether.

F is nowhere to be found, so I must redouble my research to discover Bill's weakness.

I pray that I can prevent the darkness that F saw coming. If only I had listened to him when I had the chance . . .

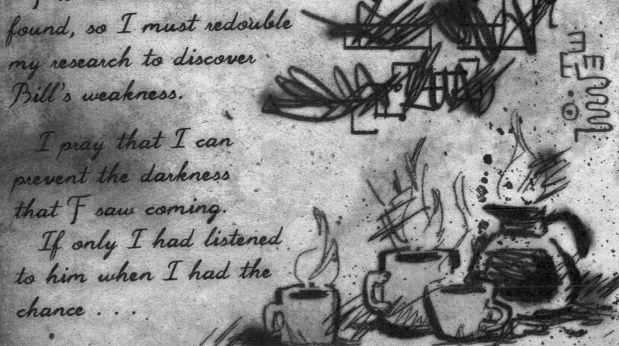

Everything I see only feeds my growing paranoia! After several weeks researching Bill, I went to town for food only to find this ➡️ mysterious symbol everywhere.

**THERE IT IS AGAIN!**

Two nights later, I glimpsed a group of hooded figures. They ran away from me yelling, "It is unseen!"

As I pursued them, I responded, "No it isn't, you creeps! I can see you just fine!" Then they threw some trash cans in my way and vanished.

Why can't I shake the idea that this new cult is somehow connected to me and my work? Can it merely be coincidence that my own project has reached this critical juncture at the same time this group has shown itself? The symbols are so familiar . . . .

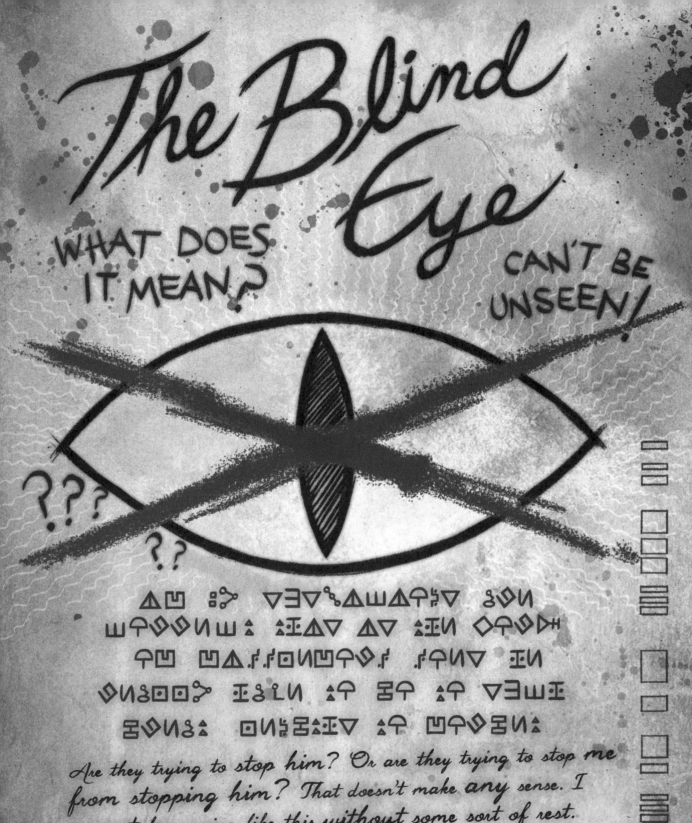

# The Blind Eye

**WHAT DOES IT MEAN?**

**CAN'T BE UNSEEN!**

*Are they trying to stop him? Or are they trying to stop me from stopping him? That doesn't make any sense. I cannot keep going like this without some sort of rest.*

*I can barely think straight.*

The folly of recording my dangerous knowledge in book form, where it can be seen by anyone, is more clear to me than ever. Despite using coded language and splitting my portal instructions among 3 volumes, I can't shake the feeling that the wrong person will read this work.

It seems to me that I need another, even more secretive way to record my thoughts, something visible yet invisible. Something I learned about in chemistry class back in college . . .

Ways
to
Hide

Even in the blackness, light can be found. My enemy can be outsmarted. Let's hope . . .

Staying awake confounds me.

To calm myself I retreated to the only sanctuary I have known over the past couple of weeks—the Triple Digits Truck Stop out on Route 14.

Their industrial-strength coffee is the best method I have for staying awake, and yet even after 6 cups I was still drowsy. A kindly looking trucker noticed that I was "having shutter trouble" and offered some suggestions to stay awake:

Pinch yourself.

Pinch someone else. They'll punch you awake.

Put peanut butter on your face and let a dog ride shotgun. (He'll lick you awake.)

Put peppers in your eyes.

Just give up, Sixer.

I blinked with a panicked start. Had I begun drifting off?

Had he really just called me . . . ?

I reared back and heard my plate of bacon crash on the floor. Everyone in the diner turned towards me, and perhaps it was just the sunrise coming in through the window, but at that moment I swear that all their eyes were **GLOWING YELLOW.**

**I SCREAMED, "GET OUT OF MY MIND, CIPHER!"** and ran towards home as fast as my weak legs could carry me. No one in this town can be trusted. He has eyes everywhere, and they are watching my every **move.**

I collapsed by the parking lot of the Twin Bed Motel. I stared at the word "twin" as I tried to catch my breath, and I realized that there was only one person left in this world that I could possibly trust with my secrets. **I began forming a plan.**

▯▯▯ ▯▯ ▯▯ ▯▯▯ ▯▯▯.

# Hiding Places

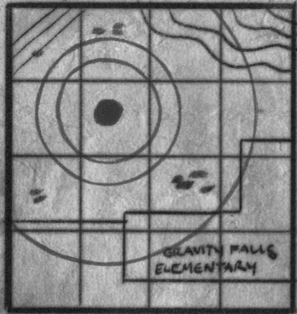

JOURNAL 2

The time for half-measures is over. If I am ever going to continue my work, then my enemy must be confronted and defeated forever! I must begin a several-day journey to the accursed caves that brought him into my life. If there is a way to destroy him, I will find it there.

But before I can begin this odyssey, I need to dispose of my journals. They're too valuable to destroy, but the information contained inside is too dangerous, and I shudder to think what might happen if they were to fall into the wrong hands. . . .

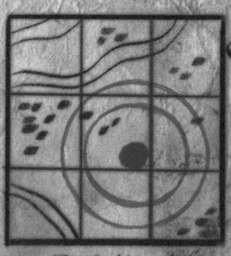

JOURNAL 1

I've already hidden Journal 2 near the elementary school. I doubt there is any child clever or conniving enough to discover it. I have another place in the woods picked out for this volume, but I've had a devil of a time figuring out where to hide Journal 1. I realized that it should be taken as far away from Gravity Falls as possible. Ideally I would take it myself, but I need to make this trip to the caves. The first snow has already fallen, and the journey will only get more treacherous the longer I delay. My former assistant refuses to speak to me, so I cannot enlist his help.

Ironically, the only other person left that I can trust is the least trustworthy person I know. He is a thief and a charlatan—but a well-traveled one. I have no doubt that he is familiar with mob hangouts and back alleys the wide world over. He will find somewhere to hide Journal 1. I have sent word to him and now must await his arrival.

Perhaps he can yet prove his worth to me.

Perhaps the mistakes of the past can be undone.

There's nothing I can do now but wait.

*I fell asleep on my cot only to awake sitting at my desk staring at the strange symbols inscribed below.*

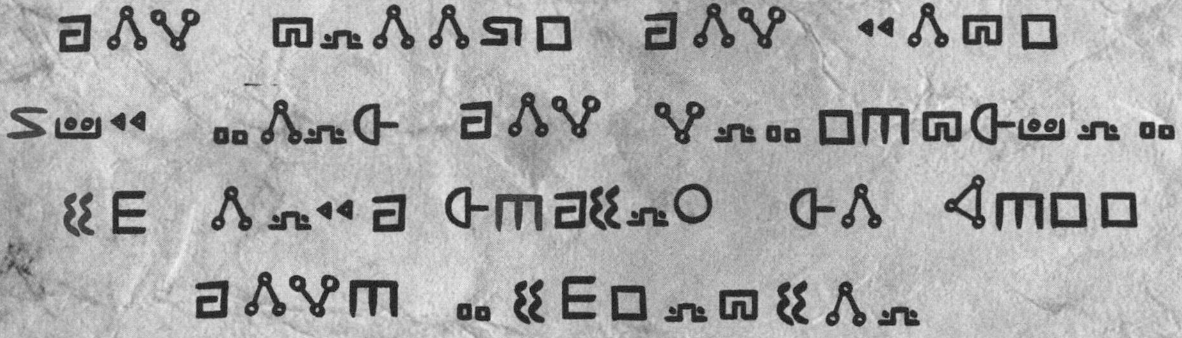

*They make no sense sideways, either.*

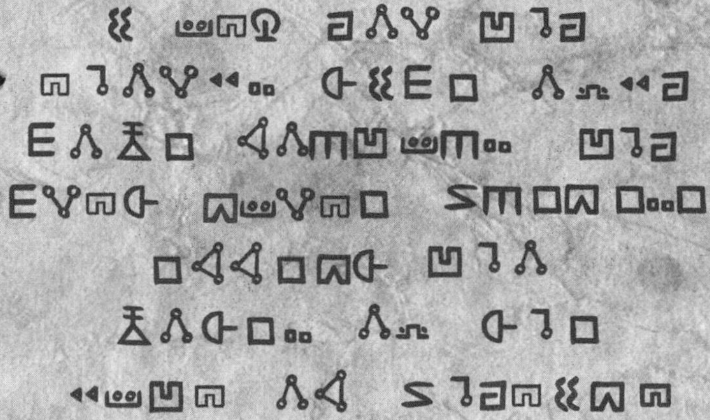

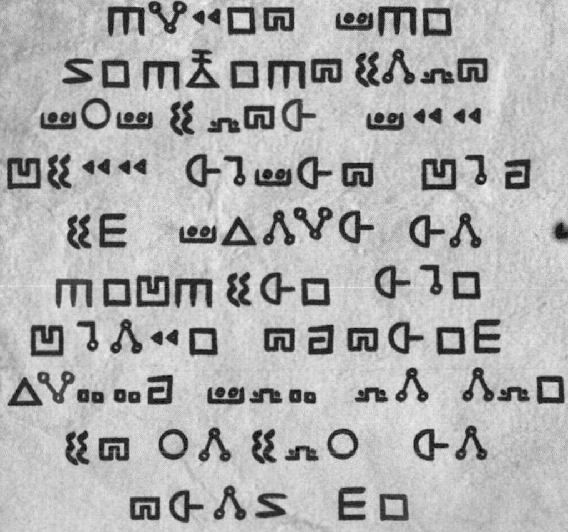

*fig. 4*

6 1 345 12 89 10 11 13 7

*He is taking advantage while I sleep.*

*Please, no!*

Unfortunately, my suspicions have been confirmed. I'm being watched.

I must hide this book before He finds it.

Remember — In Gravity Falls, there is no one you can trust.

TRUST NO ONE!

The odds that one of his agents, perhaps possessed, will access my research grow stronger.

I fear my time is running out.

So tired . . .

When I close my eyes, I see these ominous patterns and symbols. When I open my eyes, they have been written in my journal!

I am not the one drawing these!!

5

Am I??

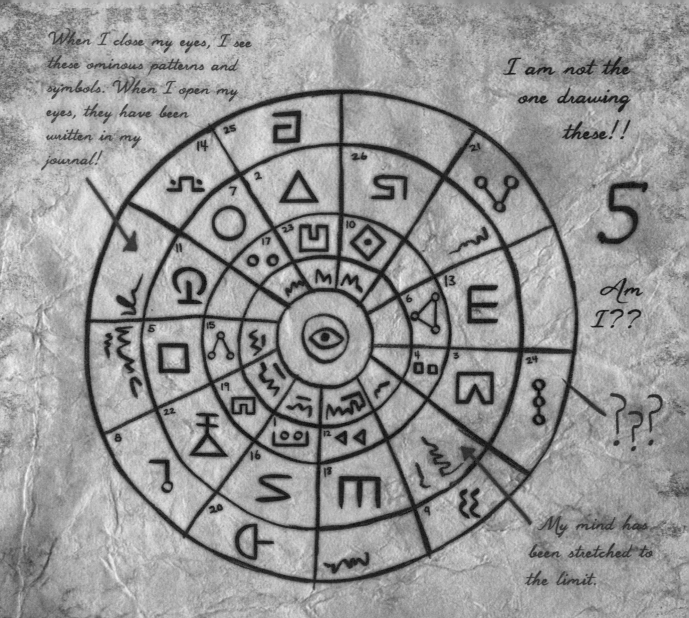

My mind has been stretched to the limit.

He's trying to control me. Trying to write in my journal during the few minutes I'm asleep. I have gambled with my future and perhaps humanity's future as well. No more writing. The time has come to bury this tome. After that, all there is left to do is wait for S. And save the world. Or lose my life in the effort.

# June 1,

~~Greetings!~~
~~Salutations!~~ ~~Whasssssup?~~

# Hey there!

My name is Dipper Pines, and from now on I'll be the one writing in this book! You're probably wondering how a normal kid like me wound up with one of the most amazing books of all time. Well, it wasn't on my summer reading list! The truth is—

~~I fought 100 mummies to get it.~~

~~I broke a vampire's neck and took it from him.~~

~~I pulled it out of the stomach of a dragon with my bare hands.~~

I . . . found it on total accident.

At first, this old thing was covered in centipedes and dust and smelled worse than my Grunkle Stan. (More on him later). But once I blow-dried all the moths out, I began to look through this sucker, and I've been obsessed ever since!

To be honest, no one in this town gets me. My weird money-grubbing great uncle just sees me as cheap labor, my sister is going through a boy-crazy phase, and the Shack employees ~~Wanda? Zeus?~~ just gossip to each other all day. No one believes me, but from the moment I arrived, I've felt like there's some conspiracy going on in this town. Whoever this "Author" is, he's the only person who ever learned the truth about this place! I vow to follow in the previous Author's footsteps, unravel the mysteries of this strange town, and answer the ultimate mystery: WHO IS THE AUTHOR? After Grunkle Stan's done making me hose off the Sascrotch, of course.

But before I begin, maybe I should tell you a little about myself!

# Your new author!

Lucky Hat!
I've worn this since the 5th grade. I can't wash it—that would ruin the luck!

Haven't slept much since I got to town. Mabel sings in her sleep, and this chilly attic bedroom creaks like a haunted ghost ship.

Trusty Vest!
I can fit pretty much anything in here! (Plus, it makes me look like I have shoulders.)

Camera!
Have one ready ALWAYS. Don't want to miss a chance to catch something weird!

Must have at all times!

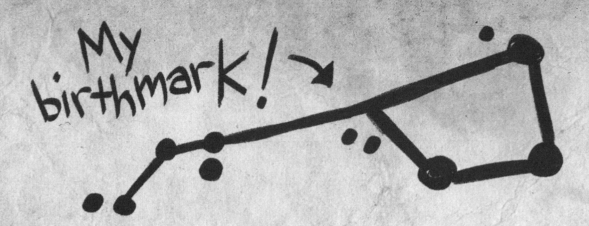

**My birthmark!** →

**NAME:** ~~M~~ Dipper Pines

**AGE:** 12 (But I'll be 13 by the end of the summer!)

**HOMETOWN:** Piedmont, California (Nice place! Very boring.)

**INTERESTS:** Video games, the paranormal, photography, ~~Icelandic pop group BABBA~~

**SIBLINGS:** My twin sister, Mabel. Imagine me with girl hair and about 1,000 pounds of sugar injected into my bloodstream. Can be a real friend when she's not doing one of her "bits." She's smarter than people give her credit for, and often acts the way she does just to drive me insane. (Was a lot more fun before her boy obsession.)

**DISTINGUISHING FEATURES:** A weird birthmark that looks like the Big Dipper (hence my nickname). Mom once said it meant I was "destined for greatness." Grunkle Stan said it looked like someone spilled hot sauce on my face.

(NOTE TO SELF: NEVER SHOW HIM THIS JOURNAL.)

# June 3,

If you go on enough road trips, chances are you've seen a certain bumper sticker ↘

## WHAT IS THE MYSTERY SHACK?

It refers to my great uncle Stan's cabin in the woods. He's transformed his house into a tourist trap filled with phony exhibits like the "Six-Pack-Alope" and the "Uni-corpse" (don't ask). None of that stuff is as weird as my sister's new boyfriend, though. He smells like roadkill and never blinks. I think I've found my first mystery to investigate—and this book will be my guide. If this guy isn't a ZOMBIE, I'll eat my hat!

# UPDATE:

He WASN'T a ZOMBIE! And I can't eat my hat because it was already eaten—by a GNOME! (I had to get a new hat at the Shack.)

Mabel and I fought an army of REAL gnomes that were posing as her boyfriend—it was terrifying but amazing!

Finally back safe and sound from one of the weirdest days in Gravity Falls.

This journal told me there was no one in Gravity Falls I could trust. But when you battle a hundred gnomes side-by-side with someone, you realize that they've probably always got your back.

Grunkle Stan told us there was nothing strange about this town, but who knows what other secrets are waiting to be unlocked? This is Dipper Pines, three-time Piedmont Middle School Spelling Bee finalist, signing off for the night.

I've always dreamed of seeing the Loch Ness monster in person, and this local legend was the next best thing! I didn't exactly get a photograph (Ugh, long story!) but here's a VERY REALISTIC drawing of the local lake monster they call the Gobblewonker!

STNLYMBL

Odd.

1) Mouth for gobbling, long neck for wonking.

2) Makes a call that sounds exactly like a beaver with a chainsaw. Seriously!

3) These enormous flippers move so fast you'd think this creature had a motor.

4) That's because it DOES have a motor. It turned out to be fake . . . but still— we did catch it. And from inside it came the REAL Catch of the Day . . .

a strange toothless hillbilly they call . . .

# Old Man McGucket

The cast on his arm has a strange hum coming from inside. He's a genius when it comes to robotics. Could he have a robot forearm? Is he slowly turning himself into a robot???

Totally wall-eyed yet he always seems to be staring at me. Very uncomfortable.

I swear that every time I look at him, the gold tooth has moved to a different part of his mouth.

Never wears shoes. He calls them "foot prisons."

Not sure what the bandage on his beard is all about. But when I reach for it, he starts to growl like a small dog.

There's definitely something suspicious about this dude, but I can't tell if he knows more than he lets on or LESS than he lets on. I wonder if the Author ever had to deal with strange locals like this guy.

# June 7,

Something extra weird happened today at the Grand Unveiling of Stan's Wax Museum of Mystery. I think I might have seen a ghost!!

Stan was telling some of his corny jokes and getting the standard audience reaction (dead silence), when I spotted a strange figure at the back of the crowd. He was bald and very pale— mostly gray and white. He was holding something in his hand, but I couldn't make it out. He suddenly ran towards the forest. There was a flash of light and he was gone.

I think he looked like this?

There is a large section on ghosts in here that I need to read ASAP. I need to be prepared in case it appears again.

Also, I'm 90% certain that "Toby Determined" is some sort of goblin. Will have to investigate.

Okay, this town just gets weirder and weirder!! Now someone has decapitated the wax figure that Mabel made of Stan. Who would want to do that??

June 8,

A jealous local artist? An ax murderer with poor eyesight? Some cursed "living wax figure"?

No. The idea of living wax figures is really dumb. I need to treat this like a real investigation!

June 9,

We solved the case!! It was . . . a group of living wax figures.

I sword-fought this unholy British → wax maniac on the roof, and would have lost if the sun hadn't come up at the right time! Also in the group were Wax Nixon, Wax Coolio, and some old Wax Man with suspenders who makes me shudder just to think about. I'm going to be sleeping with a fireplace poker under my bed from now on.

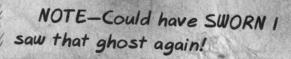

NOTE—Could have SWORN I saw that ghost again!

# June 10,

It's 2 AM and I'm giving up. There's no way to trap the thing. I don't understand how it can move so fast without any legs.

Okay, I'm tired and being unclear. Let me start again at the start.

*whisper...whisper...*

This is Dipper Pines, officially starting over.

It started right around lunch. Mabel and I had finished disposing of the wax figures. (There was a lot of melting involved. On the bright side, Mabel has some lumpy new crayons to draw with!) We were watching TV and eating some of her "world famous" Peanut Butter and Whatever Else is in the Fridge Sandwiches when I heard something in the walls. A familiar voice came through the vent, mumbling about an "exclusive interview" with a possum that was "coming up next."

That's when I knew that SOMETHING WAX HAD SURVIVED.

I tried to convince Mabel to join me in finding it, but she was busy trying out her new crayon set (she invented a new color called "BLORANGURPLE") while watching "Dream Boy High 2: Craz & Xyler's Bodexcellent Radventure," so I knew she was lost.

I knew that I WAS ON MY OWN!

I needed to go into the air-conditioning vents, but I wasn't going in unprepared.

I said goodbye to Mabel and jumped into the living room vent. The glow from the television quickly faded as I shinnied down the duct. I turned on my flashlight and was stunned to see a maze of corridors.

UGH!

I could hear the creature's voice coming from above and to the left. "They took me out of Brooklyn, but they couldn't take Brooklyn out of me." I followed it, dropping bits of bread from my sandwich so I wouldn't get lost. The duct got really narrow, but I was able to make it through. Just as I reached the top, I dropped the flashlight down the hole. I was left in complete darkness.

I heard the creature again. It was much closer.

"Do blue-eyed people see better?"

What was that supposed to mean? Was he taunting me? Could he somehow see in the dark? I crawled blindly towards the voice, dropping more bread crumbs as I went.

As I came around the corner, I could see the shape of the disembodied wax head of the Suspenders Man.

I was unprepared for what came next. As I swiped at it with my net, the head somehow jumped out of the way. I fell forward and landed hard on my elbow. The head mocked me: "There's nothing funny about the funny bone." I swiped at it again, but it came rolling at me like a bowling ball and knocked the net out of my hands. It rolled into the far corner, turned, and came at me again. I got tangled up in my rope and covered in peanut butter from my sandwich and ended up stuck in the bottom of a narrow duct. From above me, I heard, "Have a great week everybody! Good night!" And then the victorious head hopped away. It took me several hours to untangle myself and crawl back out into the living room.

**STUCK!**

I'm going to sleep right here in Grunkle Stan's chair.

# June 10,

It's 10 AM and I've been woken up by the joyful conversation between Mabel and the disembodied head. Apparently, the way to tame the thing is to let it interview you.

I'm going to go shower and wash off all this peanut butter. I could use an off-day from all these paranormal creeps....

This creep is named Gideon Gleeful, and he runs a rival tourist trap called the Tent of Telepathy. He's a fake just like my Grunkle, but he's way more dangerous—because people actually find him CHARMING! Including my sister Mabel. It's the classic story. Boy meets girl. Boy loses girl. Boy tries to murder girl's brother. Obviously we defeated him.

# This Creep

The hair. Why is it so high? Why is it so white? This kid is, like, 10 years old. Does he dye it that color??

There is no soul behind these eyes. Just unending evil.

This little pig nose is hilarious.

This amulet was no joke. Where did he get it? It gives the wearer telekinesis and a general "folksy vibe." Luckily Mabel smashed it!

He smells like a combination of baby powder, after-shave, and marshmallows.

I got to admit, this suit is pretty sharp.

He swore "eternal revenge" on us or something like that, but seriously, how scared should we be of the world's palest 10-year-old? Forgetting his name . . . NOW.

## Wendy Corduroy

Here's a name I won't forget anytime soon. Mabel & I BOTH agree she's the coolest person in town. She lets me ride Stan's golf cart and sneaks us ice cream sandwiches without paying for them. She's also really confident—even STAN seems scared of her!

Soos says she's the lumberjack's daughter, and supposedly can climb and/or chop anything, but mostly I just see her looking for ways to get out of work. She has also tried giving Mabel advice about not getting so many dumb crushes, which I really appreciate. Crushes are a waste of time. That's why I never have them. Nope. Never. Not once. ~~One time while Stan was giving us our daily chores, her elbow touched mine.~~

Oh no, she's looking at me!!

## I'M PRETENDING TO WRITE SOMETHING DOWN.

# June 14,

Just got back from an INCREDIBLE adventure at a haunted convenience store! I fought these two ghosts and beat them single-handedly! ~~I had to dress up as a~~

Never mind. Not really anything noteworthy about how they were defeated.

But Wendy and her teen friends were all really impressed. Nothing really to write about Wendy, either. I mean, what would I write, right? Right!

Okay, I'm done writing.

Well, I'm not! Dipper's gone to bed, but I need to write down what happened tonight, and I forgot the combo to my diary lock. (Again.) I can't stop thinking about

AOSHIMA

Greetings. This is Tracey (aka Dipper # 3), officially taking over authorship of the journal. Dipper # 4 (aka Quattro) and I were given the task of distracting Robbie by stealing his bike. After leaving it in the woods, we returned to the party just in time to witness "Dipper Classic" betray our Clone Bretheren. We watched in horror as he melted them with a sprinkler. Why would he do such a thing? I would never do such a thing, so how could he? He is me! Or, he is <u>we!</u> Anyway, you get the point.

Quattro and I are hiding in the bedroom closet, waiting for D.C.'s return. When the party ends & Dipper Classic falls asleep, we will put Plan C into action—we will take over his life and start dating Wendy. He will live in the closet. I've got it all worked out. It's what he would do if he was us. (Which he is.)

## Clone Schedule

| Sun | Mon | Tue | Wed | Thu | Fri | Sat |
|---|---|---|---|---|---|---|
| Quattro | Tracey | Quattro | Tracey | Quattro | alternate | Tracey |
| ~~Shower~~ | ~~shower~~ | ~~shower~~ | ~~shower~~ | ~~shower~~ | ~~shower~~ | ~~shower~~ |
| Eat* | Eat* | Eat* | Eat* | Eat* | Eat* | Eat* |
| All Day Date with Wendy ↓ | Work | Work | Work | Work | Work | All Day Date with Wendy ↓ |
| | Eat* | Eat* | Eat* | Eat* | Eat* | |
| | Work | Work | Work | Work | Work | |
| | Date w/ Wendy | Date w/ Wendy | Date w/ Wendy | Date w/ Wendy | Date w/ Wendy | |
| Debrief | Debrief | Debrief | Debrief | Debrief | Debrief | Debrief |

\* No liquids!

Just reviewed the plan with Quattro and he isn't happy with how I split up the days! He thinks it's unfair that I get Saturday and he gets Sunday. I explained to him that it all balances out fairness-wise, because I'm the one who took the time to make up this chart and figure all of this out. I mean, what has he done? Sit in the corner coloring and eating cheese crackers—that's what!

Boy, I really get on my nerves sometimes! Hey, is someone coming? Why did I write that?

OH, NO!

Original Dipper here!

I came back from the party and heard myself arguing with myself in the closet. I opened the door to find 3 and 4 inside. I was so happy to see those guys. I'd forgotten all about them! They took one look at the Pitt Cola in my hand, however, and freaked out, said "You'll never get us!", and ran out of the room and into the woods before I had a chance to explain.

Kinda worried about those dudes. It's supposed to rain tomorrow.

On the bright side, guess who just danced with Wendy???

# June 18,

Okay, so remember that un-crackable historical document that the Author puzzled over? Well, Mabel's silliness accidentally solved it! And it led us to discover that the town was actually founded by

# Quentin Trembley

### the 8th + 1/2 president of the United States.

A man so silly that they tried to erase him from history. Observations:

1) Haircut by his third wife, Sandy. (She was a woodpecker. That explains a lot.)

2) Described his measurements as being, "14 stacking-turtles in height, and forty-bleven Tremble-quarts in diameter!" No idea what that means.

3) Shouts the word "AMERICA" every 3 minutes on the minute, regardless of context.

4) Never wears pants, because: "That's what the redcoats will be expecting!" I bet Grunkle Stan would have voted for this guy.

How do we know he was the president? Dude told us HIMSELF! He kept himself alive for 150 years by encasing his body in peanut brittle! Which apparently works, although it doesn't make you smell too awesome. (Believe me.) As strange as Quentin is, he was a really nice guy, and was very grateful that we helped him escape and "didn't judge him for his radical theories about Irishmen."

To show his gratitude, he made Mabel a congressman (it's already gone to her head) and gave me THIS!

# The President's Key

—It can open any lock in America made before 1877!

—It's made from a melted piece of the Liberty Bell.

—Quentin used it to constantly barge in on Andrew Jackson while he was dressing. (Andrew Jackson hated this. He tried to shoot Quentin Trembley on 14 different occasions.)

—Can supposedly "unlock an eagle." I don't even want to know what that means.

—There's so many things I can do with this. Thinking of ransacking the Gravity Falls History Museum later!

KEEP AWAY FROM GRUNKLE STAN

Blubs and Durland told us to keep the details of our adventure with Quentin Trembley to ourselves, but we had to tell somebody! And Soos seemed like a safe bet. Boy, were we wrong.

This morning, Mabel and I came downstairs and found Soos sleeping in a giant tub of peanut brittle in the middle of the living room. He was trying to preserve himself so he could "check out the Distant Future Dudes!!" He had a straw sticking out of the peanut brittle so he could breathe, and illustrations of how he thought future technology would look.

Mabel saw a great opportunity for a prank. First, we ransacked the gift shop for some cardboard boxes, and then used up all of Grunkle Stan's tinfoil. Bam! Perfect future costumes.

Next, we taped some goat hair together for a Rip van Winkle beard to put on Soos. Then we started Stan's fog machine, turned the lights out, and threw a couple of flashing yo-yos behind the couch and hit the alarm clock.

Soos awoke with a start, and Mabel chanted, "Beep bop. Welcome to the future, Past-Man! It is the year Bleventy-Billion! Tell us your ways of the past," while I told him he had awoken from Mega-Sleep. The Cyborg People of Earth were losing Plasma War V to the Venusian/Amphibian Alliance.

I called him "The One Calculated to Save Us" and asked him to help us win "the Great War against Admiral Laser-Face."

Soos bought it HARD. He was ready to join the battle till he stepped into the hallway and saw his reflection in the mirror. He knew right away that the beard was glued on. Apparently, Soos is unable to grow facial hair. (The few hairs he normally has on his chin are glued on by <u>him</u>.)

We spent the rest of the afternoon watching "Return Backwards to the Past Again 3" and eating peanut brittle. It's too bad time travel isn't actually real.

UPDATE! TIME TRAVEL ACTUALLY IS REAL! Remember the "Bald Ghost" I kept seeing? It turns out he was the world's worst time traveler! His name was ~~Blondo? Benson?~~ Blendin, and he was as weird as he looks.

He came from the year "20͂712" to fix time anomalies, but I think he ended up causing them instead with his time tape. I wish I had held onto this gadget! I wonder if I can make my own.

# Blendin Revealed

His head catches on fire every time he time travels— and burns off all his hair!

His time goggles allow him to see the future, the past, but not really tiny print. Dude needs to switch prescriptions!

His chrono-flage suit constantly glitches, even though it's supposed to make him blend in to any surroundings. Hey, "blend in." I finally got that!

← Not a good look, honey! YIKES!

Mabel here! Dipper is over in the corner with Soos's tape measure, the kitchen timer, and some jumper cables. So while he is distracted, I thought I'd write about something way more important than a time travel adventure.

This little super hero came in and saved my life today. I never knew I was missing something till Waddles showed up and showed me I was missing a Waddles. Specifically him, Waddles, the pig. He's a best friend, best pet, and best magically transformed prince(?) rolled up into one!

# WADDLES THE SUPER PIG!!!

Super Sensitive Ears can hear someone eating from 2 rooms away.

Coal Black Eyes can see into your soul and judge whether you are worthy of his love.

Super Chunky Cheeks can withstand even the most extreme pinching from any Aunt or Granny.

His Tummy is super cute and super ticklish. Kind of his Achilles' Heel. Or would it be 'Achilles' Hoof'?

TIME DOESN'T MATTER! I WILL LOVE HIM* FOREVER! *IS WADDLES A HIM OR HER? I HAVEN'T DECIDED ON ITS GENDER YET!

AWW! HE'S HELPING!

# Rumble McSkirmish

A SUPER-POWER NINJA-TURBO NEO-ULTRA HYPER-MEGA MULTI-ALPHA META-EXTRA UBER-PREFIX NIGHTMARE!

Okay so, long story, but I kinda conjured my favorite arcade game character into the real world to try to be my bodyguard. But instead of guarding my body he punched it to a pulp! Turns out the only way to beat him is to let him beat YOU—then the game resets. I may need to reset my spine after today!

Says his name is short for "Rumble Fracas Melee Fisticuffs Slapfight McSkirmish." Claims his true name can only be spoken by the greatest of warriors. (Or anyone who "Inserts 4 Quarters Now!")

SIDE VIEW—So thin, even after eating all those tacos and power ups!

NEVER USE THIS COMBO!!

← ← P P → ← ↓
K K ↗ P (×3) K

His bandana is red because it's soaked in the blood of his enemies! Or maybe it's soaked in tomato juice? That would be less cool.

His hair is always blowing in the wind, even when there is no wind.

Eyepatch flips sides every time he turns around. I may need to write the game company to complain about this dumb animation error!

He also has this red belt. Is it also soaked in blood? This blood wardrobe thing is pretty creepy now that I think about it.

Always bare-chested. When I tried to give him a shirt to wear, he destroyed it with a fireball.

The jagged edge on his body is real, not just a bad drawing by me. He's made out of pixels—and they are SHARP!

# The Summerween Trickster

The scariest/goofiest monster we've encountered so far! And that kid isn't just there for scale. We saw the Trickster swallow him whole! I ticked him off for not having enough enthusiasm about a made-up local holiday called "Summerween" and he almost destroyed us.

1) Tall, stretchy body is the stuff nightmares (and taffy) are made of.

2) Really easily offended. If I was a 13 foot tall immortal monster I think I'd be less touchy.

3) Raspy voice, which Grenda said was "SUPER HOT!" Worried about her.

4) Can morph its body just like "Mr. Faceless" from the anime movie "The Cranky Girl Who Did Chores in Spirit Town." (Mabel has watched that 82 times.)

5) Rips his clothes every time he transforms, which explains all the stitches.

But after chasing us around town all night, he revealed his true nature to us—

The guy's made of Loser Candy! Something like, thirty <u>years</u> of Loser Candy. And all he ever wanted was for someone to eat him.

The scariest thing I saw on Summerween Eve was Soos actually eating the Summerween Trickster.

Second scariest was Stan trying to get into a girdle for his vampire costume.

BLORCH

All candy!!!

# July 6,

What a day! Stan made a bet with Mabel and she's been left in charge of the Mystery Shack (ridiculous but true).

She asked me to find a legit attraction for Grunkle Stan's tour—AND I DID IT!! I went to a spooky-looking part of the forest and built one of those tiger traps. It wasn't long before I caught something. Only one small hiccup—

I didn't dig the hole deep enough. I thought I'd catch a gnome or troll. The biggest I'd planned for was about werewolf size. I'd never have guessed I'd catch the very beast that almost defeated the Author—the GREMLOBLIN!

I slowly lowered my sack over its enormous head and the monster immediately fell asleep. (I've seen Stan use this trick on Soos, too. Put a blanket over Soos's eyes and he instantly falls asleep, like a parakeet. True story.)

I tied one end of a rope around the sack and the other to the back of the golf cart. I dragged it out of the hole and back to the Shack.

YES!! Finally! Dipper Pines: Monster Hunter Supreme!! If only Stan was here to see that I actually caught something other than a cold for once. ~~I wonder if the Author would be impressed.~~

# BodySwap!

Hello, BIG IMPORTANT JOURNAL that Dipper writes in instead of having social interactions. This is your new lord and master, MABEL! Well, actually, it's Mabel inside Dipper's body. See, there's this whole body-switching thing going on right now, but I won't bore you with all the science-y details. Let's just say that thanks to ~~magic science~~ Gravity Falls, Dip-Dip's body is temporarily under new management.

Dipper has never used a comb in his life. I tried to comb his hair and the comb got stuck! (Permanently?)

Mr. Handsome

mabel inside

I ♥ Wendy!

This outfit smells. If I don't get back to my own body soon I am going to burn it.

Moist hands. Always moist. Seriously, I cannot keep them dry. Ugh!

Made a point to never look below the chest!

## The Body of an Awkward Preteen Boy!!

On the bright side, I have a lot of newfound aimless aggression. May want to punch some things. While dancing!

While I'm in control, I'm gonna write about something that's ACTUALLY interesting: my long-distance fish-boyfriend, Mermando!

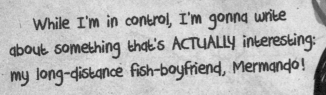

That swarthy little moustache. Hubba hubba!

Half fish and half shirtless guy. The perfect combination!

Says he has a blowhole somewhere, but the less I know about that, the better.

Supposedly has, like. 13 hearts— and all of them were breaking when he missed his family!

My first kiss! And Dipper's, too . . . hahaha

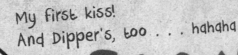

# SMOOCH

"Dipper the Monster Hunter." Hahaha!

I guess I'm not really being fair to my brother. He did save Mermando's life with that kiss. Dipper has done a lot of heroic stuff this summer and saved us all a few times. As brothers go, he's pretty much the best one I could ask for.

But giving him this awesome new room? Over my dead body!!

Or over his dead body?  Or over my dead body and his dead brain?

Never mind.

# July 11,

Well, I guess I should've seen this coming— Grunkle Stan stole a dinosaur egg from the cavern. He's hoping to hatch it and make it into an attraction. I want to be mad at his messing with nature and all, but I'm actually kind of into it. I mean, who wouldn't want to have a pet baby dinosaur??!!

But the heating lamps he's using to hatch the egg are taking forever!! Tonight, Mabel and I are going to slip the egg under Stan while he sleeps. He's got this whole creepy-old-man humidity thing going.

# July 12,

The egg hatched!!
WE HAVE A BABY DINO!!!!!
I think it's a Compsognathus.

They grow no bigger than a chicken, and they're supposed to be pretty smart as far as dinosaurs go. One thing's for sure— Compy sure loves his "Mama Stan." Little guy's been following Stan around everywhere he goes.

Waddles has taken to hiding in Mabel's bed, which Mabel actually loves, because she can make constant "pig in a blanket" jokes.

# July 14,

Turns out he's a bit too much like his Mama Stan. He picks the pockets of all the tourists with his little beak and then scares them away with a squawk that I swear sounds like "no refunds." All this would be fine with Stan if the little thief would share his ill-gotten gains. But he's gathered all his loot into a pile and sits on top of it like a dragon with a hoard of gold, hissing at anyone who comes near.

# July 15,

It took a lot of effort, but we were finally able to catch Compy. Stan tried to lure him into the cage with his gold watch. But it was like the dino could almost smell the fake gold plating. Stan had to sweeten the pot with a couple of credit cards and a twenty-dollar bill before Compy would bite.

We've given him to Farmer Sprott. He's very comfortable handling "unusual livestock." Hope he keeps his valuables in a good strong safe.

We're back from perhaps the craziest, scariest adventure yet—a trip inside

# Grunkle Stan's Mind!

We finally encountered Bill Cipher, the strange triangular brain-demon mentioned in the journal. (Although many passages that seem to reference him are incomplete or ripped out.) He was trying to steal a code in Grunkle Stan's brain, and we had to rummage through HUNDREDS of Stan's thoughts to stop him. Some of the stray memories I saw in there that I didn't mention to Mabel. . . .

Stan's Bar Mitzvah at the age of 12. His dad seemed pretty upset he was wearing Groucho Marx Glasses to the temple.

Grunkle Stan celebrating his birthday alone by watching CASH WHEEL in a gross hotel and eating "UNLUCKY LEPRECHAUN" cereal out of the box. (Apparently, his birthday is June 15th. Who knew?)

Grunkle Stan getting married?! Apparently he wedded a waitress named Marilyn Rosenstein in Las Vegas for 48 hours, but it turned out she was just trying to steal his car. (A true scam artist. Maybe she was the right one for him!)

Lots of memories of an empty swing set on the beach. What's all that about?

Stan teaching a young Soos how to box.

The most important memory was one where Stan revealed he actually cares about me. When I discovered that, it was the boost I needed to take down Bill for good.

It turns out that in the "Dreamscape" you can become anything you want. Me and Mabel decided we wanted to become AWESOME!

We sent Bill packing to wherever he came from and finally managed to escape back to reality. Unfortunately, reality turned out to be much less fun than the dream world. While we were busy in Stan's brain, Gideon somehow got control of the Shack!

We have to crash with Soos and his grandma tonight. Too tired to write much more. Going into someone else's dreams doesn't mean you get to sleep. We'll come up with a plan to get back the Shack tomorrow. I'm sure Stan has some sneaky plot up his sleeve.

I'm pretty tired, too, but I can't sleep. After that crazy adventure, and after almost being blown up by a top hat-wearing geometric shape, my nerves are all BLAHH! Plus, I'm worried about Gideon, and Abuelita's porcelain angels are looking at me super weird. I just wish I could fall asleep again, because I want to have another encounter with

MY DREAM BOYS!

I've seen them in all the "Dream Boy High" movies, and now I've seen them in person! Or inside a person—namely Stan.

 Cra2 is the cute one.          Xyler is also the cute one.

I usually associate blue hair with my grandma, but Cra2 makes it work. Work it, Cra2!

          You are rockin' that tank top, Xyler!

Did not picture Cra2 as a drummer. Seems more like a tambourine kind of guy. But the #1 instrument he can play is my heartstrings. Me-yow!

          I was ready for their visual beauty, but they also smell wonderful. Like a baby bunny dipped in bubble maker, with cupcake icing on top.

The "Dream Boy High" VHS tape series was made in the late '80s by a company called Good Enough Entertainment so their animation was sometimes kind of weird. Occasionally, their lip syncing doesn't match with what they're saying.

          Our time together was so short. I wish I could see them again, but they only appear in dreams. Oh, I guess maybe I should stop writing and start sleeping and dreaming.

Here comes Mabel, Dream Boys!!!

Oh my gosh, I am STILL catching my breath from the whirlwind adventure of the past few days. Gideon almost beat us, but then he screwed it all up in true supervillain style—with a giant robot. Mabel called it the Chubtron Loser-Droid One Thousand but I called it

# THE GIDEON - BOT!

Finally, a version of Gideon that's as big as his ego!

Gideon controlled it from inside the head. He wore this stupid black skintight onesie covered with Ping-Pong balls.

The robot version is even more roly-poly than the real Gideon. Why wouldn't you make yourself look more buff, dude?

What's with the glowing cheeks? Is this robot wearing makeup?

Who does he think he's fooling with the patriotic flag pin? The only thing Gideon is loyal to is Gideon! And Lil' Sweetykins brand baby cologne.

McGucket built it. I guess he'll invent stuff for anyone who will hang out with him. Still can't tell if he's a good guy or a bad guy.

** WEAKNESS: Punching, bravery, and Mabel's grappling hook.

Everything's back to normal now. Actually, it's better than normal. Gideon's in jail and everybody is in love with the Pines family. We were even interviewed by Shandra Jimenez on "Good Morning, Gravity Falls!" Stan spent the whole time stealing shrimp from the craft services table. Everyone seems happy.

Everybody but me. Half the summer is gone and I'm no closer to figuring out the big mysteries of Gravity Falls.

Gideon wanted this journal so badly that he risked everything to get it. Why?

I have no idea.

He asked about Journal 1. From what I've read, there are two more journals. But where are they?

I have no idea.

What happened to the Author? Is he still alive? Why are so many pages burned and ruined?

I HAVE NO IDEA!!

I'm running out of time to figure this out. No more fooling around. If I'm ever going to get to the bottom of all this, I need to find out what happened to the Author. Time to get serious. RIGHT HERE. RIGHT NOW.

Right after the grand reopening after party.
I wonder what Wendy's going to wear. . . .

I just got a huge break. A HUGE BREAK!!!!

These super-serious government agents showed up today at the Shack! They started poking around and uttering phrases like "mysterious activity" and "conspiracy of paranormal origin." Man, they were speaking my language!!

Of course, Stan gave them the brush-off and told me not to speak with them. But I've got to show them this book. Once the three of us put our heads together, we'll crack the case of Gravity Falls wide open! And after that, who knows what the future might hold?

# July 21,

The grand reopening after party was a total train wreck. There was a zombie attack (sorry, Powers and Trigger!) and Soos became a zombie! (We're in the middle of curing him right now.) But here's the real headline of the night:

## STAN KNOWS ABOUT THE MAGIC!!!

He's known ALL ALONG! I mean, he'd have to be really stupid or actually blind not to have seen _something_ after living in Gravity Falls for thirty years. But Mabel and I both bought his "clueless old man" routine.

He says that he was lying to protect us kids. Part of me thinks that there's got to be more to it than that. But Mabel believes what Stan told us, and I have to admit that he did kick a lot of zombie butt to keep us safe.

Speaking of which, I'm pretty sure that Mabel is screwing up the potion to de-zombify Soos right now.

There's no way the formula calls for whipped cream and boba balls.

# July 23,

Wow. The last few days have been more stressful than the rest of the summer put together. First we went up against a horde of zombies, and now we've faced and defeated the Shapeshifter. It almost feels like the journal itself is fighting us since I took my vow to find the Author, like it doesn't want its secrets revealed. . . .

Well that sounds super paranoid and maybe even a little insane. I'm going to bed.

Ugh. It's 3 AM and I've barely slept. Soos was right—every time I fall asleep I start having nightmares about the Shapeshifter. But it's worse when I'm awake 'cause I just start thinking about Wendy and how I confessed my feelings. I wish I could shapeshift into someone else right now. Someone having a normal summer vacation without an impossible crush on an impossible girl.

At least one good thing came out of our
encounter with the Shapeshifter:

# THE LAPTOP!

PROPERTY OF F

Soos says this thing is really old. Like super old. 1980s old.

There are some unique keys with weird symbols.
Are they in code? Magical? Alien???

Calling this thing a "laptop" is kind of a stretch. It's so
heavy it would cut off the circulation to your legs.

Who knows what information is hidden inside? If Soos can
get this thing fixed, it could be the clue that finally solves
the big mysteries of Gravity Falls!

Or it might just be filled with some classic 8-bit games.
Either way it's a win.

After the horrors of the last few days, Mabel and I decided to try to have some summer relaxation at the local mini-golf place. Bit of advice—you can NEVER relax in Gravity Falls! Instead we encountered

# The Lilli-putt-ians

## Mini-Golf MAJOR terror!

This tiny race of golf-ball people has been turning the golf course into a war zone every night for eons. Soos says he's always suspected that tiny people control mini golf, gumball machines, ATMs, and cuckoo clocks. I'm starting to wonder how many he's right about!

Delightful costumes help distinguish each golf hole's population and keep their 100-year race war going.

Look cute from a distance, but get up close and they are a pockmarked horror show!

Rubber brains inside golf ball heads make them not so smart.

Golf ball heads make them nearly indestructible.

On the bright side, they hate Pacifica as much as I do!

Mabel tried to keep one as a pet and bring him home. She named him Weensy and put him in her pocket, but he escaped by poking a hole out with a golf pencil. If my Shrinking Adventure taught me anything, Weensy will probably be caught in a jar by another curious kid soon,

***WEAKNESS: ~~A speech about working together~~ A SWIFT WHACK TO THE FACE WITH A GOLF CLUB!

24"

Whoa! Dipper and I just got back from this BIG FIGHT with everyone's least favorite triangle: Bill Cipher!

Dipper is upstairs collapsed from exhaustion—so I'll write this entry for him! An entry about a monster I call . . .

# BIPPER (BILL'S MIND + DIPPER'S BODY)

To most people he looked just like my brother. Even I was tricked at first! And I'm normally, like, SOOOO perceptive! But there're a few tips to tell the difference:

1) EYES—Look at him sideways and you can see a quick flash of scary CAT EYES (and not from the kind of cat you want to pet!)

2) HANDS—Chillingly cold. Is Dipper technically "dead" while being possessed?

3) SMILE—Unlike Dipper, he actually smiled! But he smiles CONSTANTLY and way too hard. I'd never seen Dipper's gums before this, and I never want to again.

4) PERSONALITY—INSANE. Jams forks into his arms, throws his body down the stairs, blinks one eye at a time. But he IS way more confident with girls. So, you know, plusses and minuses.

5) STYLE—Gotta give the guy props on this one. He wears this suit like a pro. Better posture than Dipper, too.

CREEPIEST OF ALL, when Stan was driving us back home, I found THIS handwritten note on the floor in the car:

NOTE to self: Possessing people is hilarious! To think of all the sensations I've been missing out on—burning, stabbing, drowning. It's like a buffet tray of fun! Once I destroy that journal, I'll enjoy giving this body its grand finale— by throwing it off the water tower! Best of all, people will just think Pine Tree lost his mind, and his mental form will wander in the mindscape forever. Want to join him, Shooting Star?

I feel like a real jerk after all this. I totally ignored Dipper's warnings, I took his journal without asking, and worst of all, I was so obsessed with my play I didn't even notice Dipper was possessed! And I of all people should know—I possessed Dipper's body once, too (Hope I never see that swap carpet again.)

Dipper, whenever you read this, I want you to know I'm sorry. And for the next week, IOU ice cream sandwiches, on me. Love—Mabel.

# GIFFANY

## A MANIC PIXEL DREAMGIRL!

'Sup, dudes! Soos here! Just had a nutzoid experience with a terrifying digital lady-monster named .GIFfany.

Since I'm the only one who got to know her all up close and personal, Dipper asked me to write this journal entry. I'll do my best, dude!

I bought .GIFfany (pronounced jiff? Or giff?) as a dating sim at BeeblyBoop's Videogames to teach me how to talk to girls better.

MY REVIEW:

1) <u>GRAPHICS:</u> Pretty nice, dude! I dig her crazy electric bow, and her eyes were mad sparkly!

2) <u>GAMEPLAY:</u> PROS—It was fun eating sushi with her, carrying her books, and watching her try on outfits!
CONS—She tried to murder me! Ha ha!

3) <u>MULTIPLAYER:</u> Not good. The moment I introduced a second player (Melody—super sweet girl, by the way), .GIFfany flew into a jealous rage! Real talk—the multiplayer mode is way better in Plumber Brothers Moustache-Kart 64.

4) <u>HIDDEN CONTENT:</u> I guess she was originally some kind of accidental A.I. that murdered her programmers and has been searching for someone to love her or die ever since. Girls are complicated, dude!

Judging the experience overall, I bought this game to get better at talking to girls, and you know what? It actually worked! So I would give this game a Soos-Score of 4 out of 5 pudding cups. Rated "E" for "EEEEEEK! She's gonna kill me!"

I do feel kinda bad about throwing her CD-ROM in the pizza oven to defeat her. I really think she's a sweet gal when she's not in murder mode. I hope she's not like, you know, dead!

# UPDATE!

.GIFfany isn't dead at all! Apparently, when her CD was sparking in the oven, her code wirelessly jumped into one of the arcade games. And you'll never guess what game she landed in—Fight Fighters!

Based on what I can see in the cut scenes, .GIFfany is trying to make Rumble McSkirmish her boyfriend now.

Although it's sort of a complicated relationship, since they keep shooting lightning and fire at each other all the time. Also I think he has commitment issues. Actually, I guess it's not that different from a lot of relationships. Except for mine!

Me & Melody are, like, a total item, dude. And not like an item that you lose and have to find again and reequip. An item that upgrades you for life! Our shared screentime over DistantChat is way better than the time Rumble and .GIFfany seem to have.

My heart bar is overflowing, dudes! Call me crazy, but I think I might marry her one day. Just don't tell anyone! Oh yeah, you're a journal. Journals can't talk!

# July 29,
# A BREAK IN THE CASE!

I've been looking for a hint about the Author's whereabouts this entire summer—but sometimes the answers are staring you right in the face!

We uncovered and defeated the Society of the Blind Eye and we owe our success to Old Man McGucket. Remember the guy I thought was just a lunatic hillbilly back during our Gobblewonker adventure? Turns out that "crazy" old man has a heart of gold and saved our minds!

But more important, McGucket used to be a brilliant scientist—specifically, the one who worked with the Author!! The 'F' the Author referred to was Fiddleford McGucket, and he could be the key to unraveling the big mysteries of Gravity Falls!!!

IF he can get his mind and memories back. There are encouraging signs—although he still does seem to like talking to raccoons. Mabel and I have hope. And we are glad to have made a new friend.

Just returned from our second trip to the future, and I'd be happy to never go back there again! The freakiest part of the whole experience?

# Time Baby

Apparently, in the future this guy rules the entire planet with a chubby dimpled fist! In the year 20712, everyone obeys him, all schools pledge allegiance to him, and he gums to death anyone who causes him trouble.

Booming voice. Surprisingly eloquent for a baby, although still says "pasghetti" and "libary."

Laser eyes that can zap you into dust. Easily distracted by jingling keys, though.

Can't walk, instead floats in this strange hover-diaper (which seems to be able to control the rotation of Earth).

Drinks "Cosmic Milk" out of a bottle the size of a skyscraper. When he is burped, it measures on the Richter scale.

Cute sausagey fingers! THAT WILL DESTROY YOU.

He can be strangely merciful when he's not going into a tantrum or making his citizens fight to the death over a time wish. He gave Blendin his job back before retiring to "NAP FOR 2,000 YEARS!" I'm sure he meant just 20 minutes. He's also responsible for Soos getting . . .

# The Infinity Pizza

A slice of pizza that Soos (and only Soos) can keep eating forever.

Regeneration!

∞

Acquired by Blendin during Globnar. (Don't ask.)

Anyone can take a bite but it will only regenerate after Soos has eaten it. This is why it can't solve world hunger—only Soos's mouth has the magic! (Did I really just write that?)

Soos can ask for different toppings and the pizza will obey. I don't know how the pizza can understand him with his mouth full.

Soos is building the pizza a triangular carrying case made out of sandalwood and leather. Looks like he's carrying the worlds tiniest, most triangular ukulele.

Grease Stain

It may be infinite, but it's also kind of greasy. Soos should have also asked for infinite napkins.

# ♡ LOVE POTIONS

Mabel here! Dipper asked me to write about love potions because he's busy hanging with the teens while they all try to cut their overpriced Woodstick admission wrist-bands off with a hacksaw.

## SOME THINGS TO KNOW BEFORE YOU TRY TO USE LOVE POTIONS!

—Love Potion is POWERFUL! It made a snake fall in love with a badger, and they're, like, natural enemies!

—Anti-Love Potion seems awful. I tasted a little bit of it, and it tasted like tears, runny mascara, and day-old ice cream eaten right out of the tub. No thanks, buster!

—WOAH—I just read the fine print and discovered something crazy! It turns out Love Potion isn't forever—it only lasts 3 hours. After that, if it ain't true love, your match will end. I guess it's more of a "nudge" than anything. Wonder how the Snadger is doing.

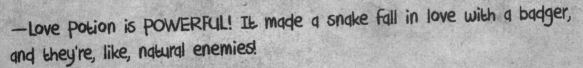

—Wait a minute . . . it's been 10 hours and Tambry and Robbie are still making out! I can see them out the window! It's totally gross—but it means their love is actually real! Maybe I AM a great matchmaker after all!

—I guess love is a mystery. Except to Grunkle Stan. He says the only true love is love of money.

# NIGHTMARE HEAD

This is what comes from Stan's love of money!

I EAT KIDS

This terrifying Gravity Falls oddity was created by Stan for once! He scared (and scarred) a large crowd of people with this thing, thinking that "all press is good press."

After this horror show crashed, Blubs & Durland shot at it for about 10 minutes to make sure it was "dead." Then children stomped on it and spat in its face. On the bright side, Robbie's parents seemed delighted by it. (They creep me out almost as much as the head.)

Note—Call me crazy, but I keep thinking I'm seeing those government agents everywhere. . . . Maybe I just feel guilty for letting them get eaten by zombies. . . .

# CATEGORY 11

# DEMONIC VENGEANCE SPECTER

So you remember how the Author thought there were only 10 categories of ghosts? Turns out he was WAY wrong! You think you've seen true terror? Check out this flannel phantom!

Ax stuck in his head from injury 150 years ago. Can pull it out and drag it along the ground to make your skin crawl.

Firey beard changes from blue to red depending on just how intense his bloodlust is at any given moment.

Aside from wood-ification powers, he can also make taxidermy do his bidding. Good thing he wasn't in the Mystery Shack—I would NOT have wanted to see Stan's displays come to life!

This ghost sure loved to talk! Mainly about his backstory with the Northwests and how they deserved to be haunted.

Except for Pacifica. The only thing stranger than meeting this ghost was discovering that Pacifica has some good inside. Sure, she's spoiled, and mean, and makes this weird face when she's annoyed, but she ended up saving me and half the town. I guess despite all her parents' attempts to make her awful, there's hope for her after all. (They ring a bell to call her like a butler and punish her with groundings and credit card cutoffs when she disobeys.)

She also looks kind of okay in an evening dress, I guess. ~~And when she hugs you she smells like champagne and flowers and... Am I crazy or was there some vibe going on?~~

The important thing is that Pacifica discovered the Lumberghost's

# WEAKNESS:

Trapping him in a silver mirror is only a temporary solution! Only a blood relative of the cursed family can defeat the specter by making amends for the family's past crimes. Pacifica showed real bravery, man.... Still getting over it!

ARCHIBALD CORDUROY

*UPDATE: Crazy thought, but I just noticed that this picture from Wendy's house looks a strange amount like the ghost.
Could this spirit have been a Corduroy...?

Stan has been ARRESTED!!

Okay, that happens all the time, but this time it's SERIOUS. Remember those government agents? Turns out they're alive and they've been watching us! They say Stan stole a bunch of radioactive waste and is using it to power a "doomsday machine" like some kind of supervillain. The Stan I know has never had any "evil plan" beyond annoying tourists.

But the more I think about it, the more I begin to wonder if Stan is hiding something. I mean, Stan has lied to us every single day since we got here. Even more troubling: last night McGucket said that the repaired laptop was showing signs of some dangerous machinery that was about to go off. Is all this connected? WHO IS TELLING THE TRUTH?!

I wish there was just one adult out there who would play it straight with me, who would tell me the truth and not lie because they think I'm too young to handle what is going on in this town. I've caught monsters, defeated ghosts, survived demonic possession, and yet still NO ONE takes me seriously enough to be honest with me!

And now Mabel and I are trapped in "protective custody," being driven to who knows where by Agent Trigger, who keeps staring at us with his weirdly intense eyes. Oh no, he just saw my journal. I hope he doesn't ta_

This piece of evidence
was taken into custody by Agent Jeff Trigger.

Case #212618

For Immediate Shipment to Warehouse B51

NOTE: Book may have evidence into the
true identity of Stanford Pines.

NOTE: Stanford is in custody and will soon be
taken to our superiors for questioning.

NOTE: My hair looks good today.
Jutston's Gentleman Gel is really working for me.

NOTE: We're totally gonna get raises for this.
No one will ever forget the bust we've done today!

# Against all odds, I'm Back

I never thought in a thousand years that I would hold this book again. The weight of it in my hands and the smell of its parchment whisks my memory back to the tragic accident that forever changed my life.

Although I was not around to record it, 30 years ago I got into a fight with my brother and was knocked through my very own interdimensional portal into a universe beyond imagination.

The last three decades have been frightening, exciting, cruel, and strange, and as I find myself back in my old study, writing in my old journal, it is hard to shake the feeling that I have awoken from a bizarre 30-year dream. . . .

How is it that I am back? It turns out that despite my warnings and the possibility of global catastrophe, Stanley managed to re-activate the portal and bring me back to my home dimension. While his intentions might have been pure, he was just as careless bringing me back as he was knocking me through in the first place. He destroyed the portal in the process, risked endangering the entire fabric of reality, and even found himself the target of a federal manhunt by the U.S. government (a logical progression from his days in the principal's office).

If it weren't for Fiddleford's memory ray, I'd likely be writing from some secret government prison by now. Fortunately, as far as the government is concerned, our encounter never happened. (Trigger and Powers will likely get déjà vu the next time they hear the words "Gravity Falls," and probably nothing more.)

But I should not dwell on the past. There will be time enough to ruminate on my years spent traveling through the dimensional rift and the strange things I saw there.

First, I must focus on the present and on the problems created by a man who is responsible for my latest twist of fate. . . .

# My Brother Stanley

## ~~HERO OR IDIOT?~~

When I first saw him, I assumed I had once again found myself in an alternate parallel dimension! Gone was the stubborn mullet-haired, frostbitten vagabond who had pushed me into the portal many years earlier, replaced by a wrinkly carnival barker with my father's face, fez, and girdle.

I'd spent the last 30 years contemplating what I might do if I saw Stanley again. Would I even be able to look him in the eye after what he did? Would I apologize for shutting him out of my life?

As it turned out, instinct took over and I punched him right in the face.

~~I feel kind of bad about that!~~

① <u>Face</u>—Inherited Dad's nose and Mom's untrustworthy tongue.

② <u>Gut</u>—I've spent the last 30 years keeping up an extensive exercise and diet regimen. Stanley . . . hasn't.

③ <u>Suit</u>—Dad's suit, which he gave me after graduation. He thought I'd wear it for my wedding. I thought I'd wear it to accept an award. Instead, Stanley has used it to trick tourists and sell key chains.

④ <u>Fez</u>—Dad's hat! He never did tell us much about the "Royal Order of the Holy Mackerel."

⑤ <u>Machinery</u>—Operated my portal like a monkey pretending to be a mechanic. Half of the instruments are held together with duct tape.

Yes, despite the extra pounds and wrinkles, Stanley is still the irresponsible, shortcut-loving overgrown child I remember from the past. Most unbelievable: his first thought upon seeing me again was to expect a thank-you—a **THANK-YOU**—after destroying my life!

Even worse, he spent the last 30 years avoiding the law by faking his own death, impersonating me, and scamming the local townsfolk with a moneymaking ruse so absurd it would even make my profit-loving father blush. Once a cheater, always a cheater. And it turns out he's become a fraud for a living. I nearly fainted when I saw what he had done to . . .

# ~~My Lab~~ "THE MYSTERY SHACK"?!

Unbelievable. Once a haven of scientific study, the cabin I built with my grant money has been transformed by Stanley over the years into a hokey freak show that mocks everything about the study of the paranormal!

① *Sign*—Designed to catch attention. Infested with owls and, for some reason, a goat.

② *Golf Cart*—Clearly stolen from a nearby Santa's Village.

③ *Tourists*—I chose this spot for seclusion, and now there are rhyming signs advertising it for 10 miles up the highway!

④ *Signage*—There are legal disclaimers in almost-impossible-to-see fine print painted up and down nearly every entryway. It's a wonder Stanley hasn't been sued yet.

⑤ *Weather vane*—The weather vane makes no sense! W, H, A, and T aren't directions! What does that even mean?!

# EVERYTHING HAS CHANGED!

My inventing room? Now a hall of ludicrous taxidermies! I mean, what the heck is a "HAM-PIRE"?!

My thinking parlor? Now a "man cave" tackier than a T.G.I. AppleRucker's Family Restaurant! My T. rex skull is being used as a coffee table!

**HAM-PIRE?!**

Even my storage room is now an overpriced "gift shop" more cluttered than Pines' Pawns! A tourist asked me if she could get a discount on a "Burpin' Stanford Pines" figurine, since it wasn't "burpin' loud enough."

These are the bane of my existence. I gathered them up and burned them immediately.

Walking around my old lab, I feel like a dead man's ghost haunting a strange fun house mirror version of his past life. I resolve to take back my home and rebuild the life that Stanley has taken from me. But I must wait until the summer is over, for the sake of the summertime newcomers I find living and working here. My impressions of them are as follows.

BURPIN' STANFORD PINES™

STANFORD

# ~~Zeus~~ "Soos"

Upon first seeing this specimen, I believed him to be one of the hairless gopher people of the dimension Rodentus 7. I was shocked to discover that he is actually a human adult man.

Quarantined him for testing due to exposure to portal radiation.

## Findings:

1) Hair growth appears in strange, awkward patches. Is he a man? Is he a baby?

2) Evidence of autolysis suggests that he survived a zombie bite. When I brought this up, he laughed and said, "That was one crazy party, dude."

3) Giggles when prodded.

4) Seems to have consumed a nearly **INFINITE** amount of pizza.

That, of course, is impossible. I may need to recheck my instruments. The strangest thing about him is his utter idolization of my brother Stanley.

~~That mark on his shirt is so familiar...~~

**RODENTUS 7**

7

# Wendy Corduroy

I recognized the name instantly! Stanley's other hired helper is the teenage daughter of "Boyish Dan" Corduroy, the local lumberjack who helped construct my lab back in the 1980s. (I hear he's grown quite a bit since then.)

Soos had apparently told her everything about me by the time we met. She was so unfazed by seeing me that she simply said, "Sup, Stan Two?" and started casually typing to her friends on one of the computing phones that seem so popular in the present.

## COMPUTING PHONE

This gadget can do everything from sending a picture of a winking cat face to ruining a celebrity's career in seconds. I'll stick to my typewriter and rotary dial, thanks.

Wendy complimented my turtleneck in a way that didn't seem sincere. I worry that she is appreciating me ironically.

~~That ice bag . . . am I losing my mind?~~

# Mabel Pines

At least there is some **GOOD** news: I am a great uncle! (Or "grunkle," as Stanley seems oddly insistent on saying.) Apparently, Sherman Pines's grandkids have been staying with Stanley for the summer. (It's hard to believe the parents would trust these kids with Stanley; they clearly thought he was **ME!**)

I was instantly charmed by Mabel's enthusiastic attitude, although a little hesitant about her utter fascination with my 6th finger. (She has already started making me finger puppets despite my requests for her not to.)

Kdv wkh idprxv "Slqfh Kdlu Fruov"

After getting her to calm down for a moment, I eventually subjected Mabel to the same testing as Soos and found her to be an odd specimen as well.

1) When I asked her to say "ah," she screamed for a whole minute and coughed up glitter. Not normal.

2) Shares the family sweet tooth. Diet seems to consist solely of items with the word "gummy" in them. I will need to discuss nutrition with Stanley.

3) Apparently knits a new sweater every day. I may request her help in repairing mine.

4) I gave her several different Rorschach tests to make sure she wasn't psychologically damaged by our experience with the portal. Here's how she interpreted the inkblot designs:

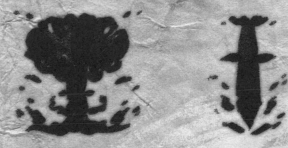

**BUNNY**  **LOLLYPOP**  **FRIENDSHIP WAND**

These interpretations are . . . unusual.
I may need to do further psychological testing.

# Dipper Pines

Twins run in the family! Although unfortunately that is the only family resemblance I see in this overly-eager, unusually sweaty ~~10-year-old~~ 12-year old. Every time I made direct eye contact with this fretful child, he started gagging like he was going to throw up, and when I tested his heart rate for side effects of dimension fever, I found it going a mile a minute. The only thing I could glean from his stammering was that, shockingly, HE was the one to find Journal 3's hiding place in the forest! (I'm not sure how accessing my journal was even possible. The only explanation is that the circuitry must have become unstable over time and perhaps water damage loosened the machinery.)

HEART RATE

Although I'm grateful to have my journal back, a quick look through reveals that he has been treating this important scientific document as his own personal diary and generally scribbling over my work with his own notations. I will have to review when I have a moment to survey the damage.

Observations:

1) Constantly sweating. Perhaps he takes after Stanley.

2) Fidgeting suggests he may still be recovering from shock of portal contact.

3) Very thin limbs. Almost noodle-y. Were his bones weakened by exposure to portal radiation?

4) Rank odor. Clearly hasn't bathed recently. Stanley should never be put in charge of children!

5) Refused to take off his hat. That hat . . . this is far more than a coincidence. The sense of déjà vu I get looking at these symbols is overwhelming.

The cave writing I saw many years ago said that these symbols (and others) had the power to bring about great change—but so many prophecies and legends turned out to be Bill's lies. Could this just be another one of Bill's tricks? How well did the ancient people of Gravity Falls truly understand Bill's power? And what are the odds that this randomly assorted group could have anything to do with my destiny?

I must not give this too much thought. The time for ancient superstitions is past. I must focus on scientific ways to address the troubles I fear are coming. . . .

# The Rift

I was dismantling the portal for good and salvaging what parts I could for future experiments when I made a horrifying discovery. Although I thought the dimensional gateway was permanently closed, I found at my feet a small tear between worlds, sparking and hovering a foot above the ground. In a panic, I scooped it up in a mason jar like it was a mosquito, and was able to create a temporary containment unit. It is just as I feared: apparently, Stanley's reckless use of the machine overtaxed it and ripped a tear in the dimensional fabric—the same way an overheated oven might burn a hole in kitchen linoleum. I had to contain it!

Rift—A glittering window into the chaos I thought I'd escaped forever. If you hold it up to your ear, it sounds like mocking laughter.

Base—
I could really use Fiddleford's help in stabilizing this. I wonder what's happened to him after all these years? When I asked, everyone abruptly changed the subject.

Containment dome—
A house for the Rift. Admittedly, I was inspired by the snow globes in Stanley's gift shop. (I must keep this away from Mabel, considering how many snow globes I saw her break in an hour.)

The path before me is clear. The world is safe from Bill Cipher as long as the rift remains contained. But I fear my device will not be strong enough to hold these cosmic forces at bay forever. I must remain vigilant and stand watch, lest trouble arise again. And if I've learned anything from a life of misfortune, it's that this is a burden I must shoulder alone.

When I tried to share my burdens with Fiddleford, it destroyed our friendship and took its toll on his mental health.

When I tried to share my burdens with my brother, he knocked me into the portal, separating me from my home for 30 years.

And after all those years in exile, living across multiple dimensions, there are precious few beings that I feel comfortable calling a "friend." What are the odds that in this one dimension, I can find someone who understands me or what I've been through?

No. The life before me is one of constant solitary vigilance against the unimaginable insanity that is Bill Cipher. I brought him into this dimension, and I'll take him out. If it's the last thing I do.

I can't believe I'm writing this, but today I actually had **FUN**. My grandnephew Dipper literally fell out of the sky and reminded me that, even in dire circumstances, one must take joy in the simple pleasures of life.

In this case, that simple pleasure is my favorite board game of all time—Dungeons, Dungeons, & More Dungeons by Ball Way Games (copyright 1974). Stanley always mocked my love of this game, and even some of my college friends called it "Girlfriend Repellant." But apparently, Dipper shares my love of a good game.

He's setting up the game as I write this. Wait till he sees my . . .

# Infinity-Sided Die

Infinite sides mean infinite outcomes. But you'd be surprised how often you roll a 4.

This thing has saved my life 3 times and endangered it around 20.

Available in infinite colors. But only 2 sizes.

Exists in a state of quantum uncertainty. Don't stare at it for too long unless you want a headache!

One time I rolled it and the sky permanently changed color. Luckily, that was in the Land of the Blind Dimension, and no one noticed (although their one-eyed king did seem annoyed).

Obviously it's too dangerous to use in a simple game of D & D & More D, but what could be the harm in just showing it to Dipper?

Well, the harm in showing it to Dipper turned out to be quite large. During one of our games, my hotheaded brother got his hands on it and accidentally conjured this jerk.

# Probabilitor the Wizard

<u>Full Name:</u> Probabilitor Pythagorus Decimaldore the 3.1415th

Claims that his staff is powered by "pure math," but I'm guessing it's just a lot of D batteries.

Mainly makes annoying math jokes. He said "Algebra Kadabra" at one point, and everyone booed loudly.

Believes that eating brains makes you smarter, which is a really dumb idea for someone who never shuts up about having a master's degree.

His henchman is much too good-looking to be pure elf. They are typically much shorter and way uglier. His ugly elf dad must have married up.

Out of all the wizards I've ever encountered, (and that includes Blandalf the Boring from the Unremarkable Dimension), this one was the most insufferable!

# WEAKNESS:
~~BLASTER GUN~~
# BEING OUTPLAYED!

As formidable as Probabilator seemed, I'm proud to say that the Pines family was able to beat the wizard at his own game. Stan's contribution was (of course) to cheat our way to victory, but Mabel's ~~disturbing~~ extraordinary imagination proved to be invaluable as well. When we needed a means of escape, she thought up something called a Centaurtaur (which is actually quite incredible if you don't pause to try to figure out how it eats . . . among other things).

**DON'T THINK TOO HARD ABOUT IT**

7
2
3

But after I fought ogres and elves alongside him, it was Dipper who impressed me the most. Pondering our adventure and the bond we shared over the game, I finally took it upon myself to read the entries he'd made in this journal.

20

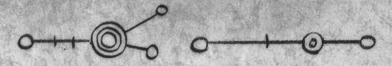

I don't mean this lightly when I say I was floored by what I saw. Instead of the aimless aggression of a typical adolescent, I discovered the same obsession with the supernatural as myself. Page after page, I read on as he navigated beasts, evaded villains, defeated ghosts (twice!), and even took down a Gremloblin. Sure, he's rough around the edges (and prone to romantic distraction), but he possesses bravery, cleverness, imagination, and drive far beyond his years.

More surprising still, he has a birth deformity—just like me! To say that I felt like I was reading about a younger version of myself is an understatement. I always thought I was the odd member of the family, but perhaps I truly have found a kindred spirit.

I presumed that there was no one on this Earth who I could consider an ally and friend. I may have been wrong.

Trusting in someone new is not coming easily. I told Dipper about the rift. But when he asked me where I've been for the last 30 years, I had no idea how to begin or what to reveal. I've been trying not to think about it, but perhaps writing about some of it here will help me get my thoughts in order. Perhaps it's time I finally reveal . . .

# My Journey

I remember those first moments after I was cast into the portal like it was yesterday. The sudden feeling of weightlessness, the helpless terror, knowing that I would soon face whatever mysterious horror had driven Fiddleford to madness.

As I felt myself being sucked away from my home (a dimension I would come to learn is referred to in the multiverse as 46'\\), I held my breath and accepted that this could be the end.

As luck would have it, it was only the beginning. I found myself sucked through the door to the place Bill had designed the portal to access, a place he screamingly refers to as . . .

# THE NIGHTMARE REALM

The dimension between all dimensions . . .

The in-between space . . .

The King of Nightmares . . .

Gateway to other worlds . . . .

Swimming through a gravity-free sea of
lightning and swirling colors, I reached
into my pocket for a spare pair of
glasses (always handy, considering
how often I break them) and found
myself staring at, quite literally, a living
nightmare.

Bill's universe is not exactly a dimension, but
rather a boiling, shifting intergalactic foam between
dimensions—a lawless, unstable
crawl space between worlds
that only the strangest and most
unknowable beings call home.
The portal closed behind me, and
I found myself trapped
there, possibly for eternity.
Before I had a moment
to properly panic over my fate,
I realized that I was hovering
before Bill, who perched on a
bizarre throne
made of optical
illusions flanked by an army
of strange and shadowy beasts.

"LOOK WHO DECIDED TO PAY ME A VISIT!" he shrieked, his voice echoing through infinity. "CARE FOR A GAME OF INTERGALACTIC CHESS? THIS TIME, YOU'RE THE PAWN!"

He snapped his fingers, and one of his beasts, a 60-foot-tall ball of fingers and teeth, let out a howl like a humpback whale and charged at me, fingers and teeth wiggling and gnashing! I managed to hide behind an asteroid field in the nick of time as the monstrosity passed me by, and I swam through the air in a panic as multiple beasts tore through the space rocks, searching for me.

Fleeing for my life, I miraculously managed to make shelter in the crater of a large passing asteroid as the monsters swarmed by. Hidden deep within the recesses of the stony caverns, I could hear Bill's shrill voice:

"SIXER WANTS TO PLAY HIDE-AND-SEEK! FIRST ONE TO FIND HIM AND BRING HIM TO ME GETS THEIR OWN GALAXY."

It was followed by the manic laughter of creatures large and small racing off to locate me. I was so crazed from fatigue and rage that my first impulse was to give myself up to Bill so I could curse him right to his face. Fortunately, before I could do anything crazy, I discovered that I was sharing my cave with a shivering family of intergalactic refugees.

# THE REFUGEES

Huddled around a strange glittering purple fire, these bandaged, war-torn creatures beckoned me near and told me their tale.

Apparently, they were asteroid miners whose ship was sucked into a dimensional wormhole, and they found themselves lost here like me. (When things in the multiverse go missing, they usually end up here.) When I mentioned Bill, they shrieked and covered their ears like I had said something obscene.

Their leader, a hairy, snaggletoothed mix between a guinea pig and a pirate, explained that my old "Muse" is actually one of the most feared beings in the entire multiverse. Bill took over the Nightmare Realm as a hideout for him and his cronies, but because this place is lawless, without any consistent physics or rules, it is eventually fated to self-destruct. This is why Bill seeks a new, more stable dimension to take over and a foolish mind willing to let him in. A foolish mind like mine.

I explained to them my history with Bill and my desire to destroy him for what he's done.

Although they were skeptical, the creatures took pity on me and offered help. They gave me one of their dimensional translators and some rations.

DIMENSIONAL
TRANSLATOR
MODEL K127X

I asked them the odds of ever making my way home, and they said they were slim. So a plan began to form in my mind. I would travel from dimension to dimension, learning what I could about Bill—his weaknesses, his secrets. I'd gain my strength, bide my time, and once I was ready, I would return to the Nightmare Realm and destroy him once and for all. I might never see home again, but at least I could save the multiverse from his wrath, and wreak vengeance for the life he stole from me.

The creatures cheered me, shouting, "Praise the Axolotl!" (I have no idea what that means), and waved goodbye as I left their asteroid and swam to the nearest wormhole, casting my fate to the wind to discover what new worlds awaited me.

# My Travels

So I embarked on a 30-year adventure—a perilous journey through the multiverse to learn what I could about Bill in the hopes of defeating him. In the process, I had many experiences that my younger self might have described as "swashbuckling" if not for the constant nausea that accompanies dimension-hopping! It feels almost as though I lived 100 different lives in those dimensions. I traveled with bandits, learned to speak 13 languages, got in a fistfight with a talking chair, and got tattoos with a tribe of octopus-armed warrior piglets.

WHY DID I GET THIS TATTOO?

HEY NOW I'M AN ALL STAR!

(These tattoos rank among my most serious regrets. Let's just say I wear this turtleneck for a reason.) I studied ancient texts, compared notes with scholars, dined with monsters, and was briefly made king of the Finger Dimension, until a 7-fingered man showed up and I lost my status.

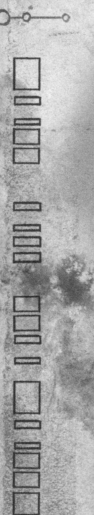

Thanks to my quick wit (and dimensional translator), I was able to talk my way into and out of food and shelter—although a number of dimensions consider me an outlaw to this day. Ironically, in the multiverse I'm just as wanted as Stanley! But my crimes had a noble purpose: I only stole supplies to work on my Quantum Destabilizer, which proved to be one of the most difficult inventions I've ever worked on. To fully chronicle my adventures would take 10 volumes, but here's a catalog of some of the most outlandish dimensions I saw. . . .

# The M Dimension

No, my niece Mabel did not draw this. This is what it really looks like.

Ugh! Writing about this place after all these years has brought back to life the extreme frustration I felt while I was trapped there. The whole reality offended my ordered and scientific mind. I mean, how does it even make sense for a vacuum to be designed like this??

If you think that's dumb, try looking at their alphabet: it's just the letter "M" 26 times! Why does a universe like this exist? Why did I have to spend time there? Why did they keep telling me to "mave a monderful mime!"?

Even though I was feeling "muicidal" after just 10 minutes there, at least they were relatively kind to me, considering how strange I must have looked to them. Not like the people in the Symbol Dimension. Those guys are @$$&@!!s.

# The Do-Over Dimension

Also known as the Yo-Yo Dimension and the Go Insane Because Nothing Gets Done Dimension (the last name being the most accurate but the least poetic). This is a world where time moves both forward and backward in a seemingly random manner. So you may have a really crummy week but then get a chance to do it all over again. Or just as you complete high school, you may live backward all the way to kindergarten.

The Do-Over Dimension can move forward normally for really long spans of time or "yo-yo" back and forth several times in one day. Professional "timelineologists" are like weathermen who try to accurately predict "what the time will be like" on any given day.

As the old saying here goes, "one step forward, infinite steps back, then two and a half steps forward, for no discernable reason."

The main problem with the Do-Over Dimension is that you remember every time you relive each section of your life. This may sound great at first—who hasn't wanted a chance to "do over" some aspect of their life? But let's see how it actually plays out . . .

TIME 1 It's been 6 months since you moved into your first apartment and things have gotten pretty messy. And now you've only got 2 hours to clean up before your new girlfriend sees the place for the first time.
RESULT 1 She is horrified at the mess and leaves early.

### BUT TIME REVERSES!

TIME 2 It's been 5 1/2 months since you've moved into your first apartment and things have gotten pretty messy. But you've got 2 weeks to clean up and redecorate before your new girlfriend sees the place for the first time. It's a lot of work, but you make the place into a palace.
RESULT 2 She asks you to marry her.
### BUT TIME REVERSES!

TIME 3 It's only been 5 months since you've moved into your first apartment. It's as messy as before and you remember how much work it was to get it in shape last time. You're not really ready to go through all that again. You do a basic cleanup and get some new curtains.
RESULT 3 Meh.
### BUT TIME REVERSES!

TIME 4 It's only been 1 day since you've moved into your first apartment. Everything is still in boxes and you don't even have a girlfriend yet.
RESULT 4 You decide to leave everything in boxes and play video games all day.

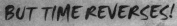

# Lottocron Nine
## (The Gambling Dimension)

It's like the mob took over the entire galaxy. Except there is no mob, because gambling is not only legal here, IT'S MANDATORY!!

Cynn City—
Central Governing
Authority of the
Gambling Dimension.
It lands on whatever planet
wins the yearly lottery to host it.

*Lzrq pb Lqilqlwb qlh khuh!*

Every aspect of life is left up to chance in this dimension.

Babies learn to roll dice before they learn to walk, and no one over the age of five goes anywhere without their lucky deck of cards. Even choosing your soul mate is left to Lady Luck.

Luckily, the government is effective. The Galactic Senate meets at the track every Saturday to ~~debate~~ bet on their favorite laws. Stan would have loved this place, but it just made me depressed. Although I had a good run in the Gambling Dimension, the dimensional bouncers ended up kicking me out for counting cards! What are the odds?

My quest to defeat Bill led me to a strange world that I mistakenly believed to be his birthplace:

# The Two-Dimensional Dimension

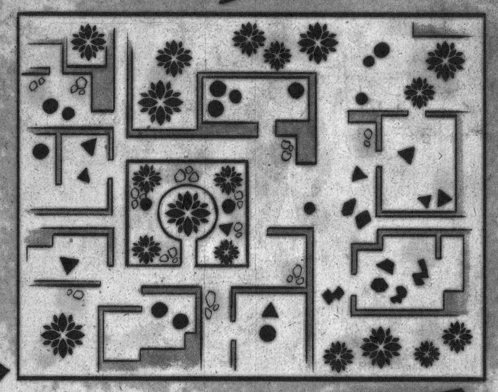

A residential neighborhood in the 2-D world (a.k.a. Exwhylia) as seen from above. ("Above" being a direction that they know nothing about and does not exist.)

This drawing approximates how my 3-D body intersected with their 2-D universe. Looking at this picture, you might think me a god in their world—but not so much.

This is what the world of Exwhylia looked like to me while I was there.

A.     B.     C.     D.

My 3-D eyes were worthless in their 2-D world! There is no sky above them and no sun to bathe them in directional light and create shadows! But here's how the Exwhylians would interpret the objects above:

A. = ● An upper-class circle.

B. = ▲ A lowly triangle.

C. = ☐ A building off in the distance.

D. = ✤ A leaf 5 inches from your face.

I believed Bill came from a similar world that was mysteriously destroyed. But how? I didn't have much time to investigate. The Exwhylians considered me to be an "Irregular" shape, which is vulgar in their society.

I was unable to explain myself, since my mouth was stuck outside their world, and I soon found myself under attack. Though small, the Exwhylians' bodies are razor-sharp, and several hundred of them began slicing into my head. Luckily, I was saved by one of the most extraordinary creatures I've ever encountered . . .

0100001 1010

# The Oracle

I was suddenly sucked out of the 2-D dimension, and I blacked out. When I awoke, I found myself in a strange mountaintop shrine surrounded by clouds, looking up at a 7-eyed creature, Jheselbraum the Unswerving.

⌖⅂ᗁ  ⊽⅀⅀⊽⅁⊽⅃ᗁ  ⊊⊔  ⅁⊿⊿⊙⊙

She told me I was in Dimension 52, and that she had been treating my wounds for a long time. Strangely, she seemed to already know my name and what my mission was.

DIMENSION 52

Whether she was psychic or had just read my wanted poster is hard to say. But she had some stunning insight about Bill. She said that if I truly wanted to face him again, I would have to protect my mind—and that she could help me, but it would require putting a metal plate in my head with difficult surgery. Maybe it was the thin mountain air, but I agreed instantly.

For a week, as I recovered, we had many long conversations about Bill. Apparently, his thirst for power caused him to destroy his home dimension—including his parents and everyone else he'd ever known. She spoke of him without anger, but with a calm, steely, clinical resolve to see his reign of terror end. She looked deep into my eyes and said I had the face of the man who was destined to destroy Bill. I was so excited that

PLATE X-RAY

we spent the entire night partying and drinking Cosmic Sand—the very same kind Time Baby himself consumes. When I awoke the next morning, she was gone and I was in another dimension entirely. It was time to continue my quest.

I sometimes wonder where she is now & how she knew so much about me. . . .

# PARALLEL EARTH DIMENSIONS

Unlike the dimensions I've already described, many dimensions in the multiverse are "parallel Earths," very similar to my dimension, but with a few major differences.

There are parallel Earths where dinosaurs still rule (one way or another).

And ones where dolphins (rather than *Homo sapiens*) took over as the dominant species after the dinosaurs went extinct. (These dolphin Earths invariably have the best water parks.)

There's a dimension where all music is just screaming, one where tennis balls chase dogs, and one where everyone is the same—except they're all babies. I didn't linger there too long—I don't care for being spit up on.

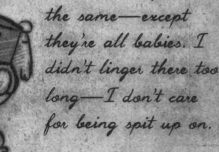

# A Better World

But after nearly 30 years of dimension-hopping, I came upon a parallel Earth almost identical to our own. There was at least one crucial difference.

On this Earth, I was never pushed into the portal by Stan.

On this Earth, my brother listened to me and took Journal 1 away from Gravity Falls.

On this Earth, I reunited with Fiddleford, and together we created a Dimensional Vortex Neutralizer that allowed us to use the portal without any risk of a connection to Bill's Nightmare Realm.

By the time I visited this parallel Earth, my parallel self was a celebrated star of the scientific community, and my small cabin in Gravity Falls had become the sprawling International Institute of Oddology.

Like a moth to a flame, I was drawn toward the Institute. Luckily for this particular Earth, I ran into Parallel Fiddleford before encountering my parallel self. He quickly recognized that I was not his Stanford Pines, and had me detained by campus security.

I put up quite a fight, but when I finally calmed down, PF explained why he was holding me captive. A few years back, he had been leading a portal expedition to a particularly dangerous dimension when one of the security officers ran into his parallel self. As soon as they touched hands, the entire dimension began to warp and fizz with static. Fiddleford and the rest of his team escaped back to their own dimension, but that officer was never heard from again. In fact, that whole dimension has ceased to exist.

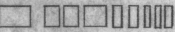

As much as I might have wanted to revel in my parallel self's success, it was clear that there was literally no place for me in this dimension. Even if I could have stayed there for the rest of my days, my own conscience would not have allowed it. I still held onto the vow I had made close to 30 years earlier to destroy Bill Cipher.

When I mentioned my vendetta to PF, his knee began to bounce with agitation and excitement, the same as my own Fiddleford's knee. Although his dimension was safe from Bill, he understood the threat Cipher posed to the wider multiverse. He was anxious to help in any way he could.

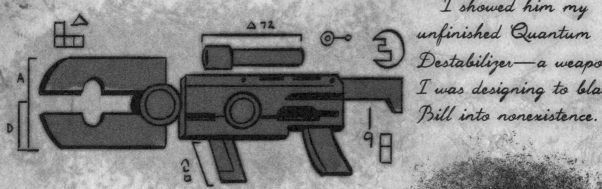

I showed him my unfinished Quantum Destabilizer—a weapon I was designing to blast Bill into nonexistence.

The problem was the power source. In all my travels since leaving Jheselbraum, I had never come across an element that had both the necessary power and the required stability.

PF suggested an element that he had discovered in the Paradox Dimension. It was inert when visible, but highly radioactive when hidden. He called it NowUSeeitNowUDontium. (A unique flair for language was something else he had in common with my Fiddleford.)

After just a few days of tinkering and minor adjustments to my blaster's design, the Quantum Destabilizer was finally finished.

I was ready to face Bill.

# MY RETURN TO THE NIGHTMARE REALM

was something that I had planned in my head for so long that it was difficult to believe it was actually happening. Plus, there are dimensions where everything happens in your head, so it can get confusing.

But there was no mistaking the Nightmare Realm for another dimension. The constantly shifting kaleidoscope of color, lack of gravity, and persistent smell of burnt hair were all signs that I was in the right place.

And of course there was also the fact that Bill Cipher instantly spotted me and unleashed his goons.

Although I was 30 years older than the last time I had faced these monsters, I was a fair bit more fit and agile.

Also, having a death ray in my hands did have its advantages.

# QUADRANGLE  OF QONFUSION

With his henchmen in disarray, I had what would probably be my only chance to attack Bill directly. Cipher sensed that, for once, momentum was not on his side, and so he retreated to something called the "Quadrangle of Qonfusion."

I only had minutes till Bill's forces regrouped, and it would take me hours to untangle the unreal architecture of his fortress.

Then I realized that in the Nightmare Realm, you did not need to follow the rules of physics, and I lunged right at him.

The moment I had worked towards and struggled for all those long years had finally come. I had Bill Cipher in my crosshairs!

But at that moment, the entire Nightmare Realm shook as the portal was reactivated!!!

There was no time to question why or to curse my luck. Bill was incapacitated with laughter, but I needed to beat the rest of his hench-monsters to the portal or my home world would be invaded by Bill's forces.

I ran along the length of the Quadrangle, and as I approached the edge, I jumped up in the air while simultaneously tossing a concussion grenade behind me. The force of the blast catapulted me past Bill's demonic gang and through the portal.

The passage between the two dimensions collapsed behind me. I reentered the world of my youth to face a brother I had not seen in 30 years. My frustration was indescribable—once again, my brother's actions had sabotaged everything I had ever worked toward.

My resolve to defeat Bill has never been stronger.

# NIGHT MARES &

Last night I awoke covered in sweat—and not just because I slept in my clothes. Bill Cipher has decided to pay my mind a visit once more. Although the metal plate I got installed in my head prevents Bill from being able to access my thoughts directly, he can still haunt my dreams. Last night, he appeared to me in a wheat field, cackling about the end of times and saying that I will be powerless to prevent his reign!

Our family is in danger, and I have to do something about it. I have been hesitant, however, to talk to the rest of the Pines about Bill (even Dipper, who I've grown to trust). I'd like to believe that this is out of a desire to protect them, but if I'm honest with myself, it's because I'm ashamed. . . .

# DAYMARES

What would they think of me if they knew that it was my folly, my hubris, that conjured Bill in the first place? That he tricked me into creating the portal, and that the rift is a direct, physical reminder of the terrible deal I made so many years ago? Would Dipper still look up to me—or would he just consider me a fool?

No, I need not tell them everything. Just enough for now. In the meantime, I have sent Mabel on an errand to see if she can retrieve some unicorn hair to protect the Shack from Bill's influence. It's a long shot, but it's worth a try.

# UNICORNS!!

Hey there! Mabel here! I just got back from a CRAY-CRAY encounter with some unicorns, so Grunkle Ford asked me to write a journal entry about them. He said I'm possibly the only person who's ever defeated one, so I guess I'm basically an expert now? **Whaaat?**

The main unicorn I dealt with was named Celestabelleabethabelle. (Pretty sure I spelled that wrong.) She was supposed to tell me if I was pure of heart, but instead she just made a bunch of junk up and was super rude. Turns out that unicorns aren't anything like in storybooks—so here's a handy guide to FACT vs. FICTION of unicorns! (To make it more horselike, I'm calling it YAY vs. NEIGH.)

**YAY!**

IN STORYBOOKS . . .

1) Their horns are supposed to determine whether you are worthy of their friendship, and shoot lasers at you if you aren't!

2) Eyes should sparkle with a million stars, even during the day when that makes no sense.

3) Lick their necks and they taste like your favorite flavor in the world!

4) They love to go on quests and will happily accompany you and a bumbling wizard companion on an animated PG adventure for the whole family.

5) Are always "The Last One."

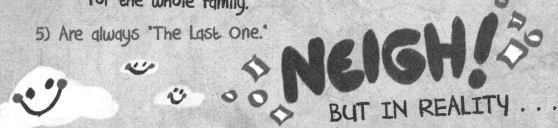

**NEIGH!**

BUT IN REALITY . . .

1) Horns just play rave music, and not even the good kind. Barely danceable!

2) Spends, like, 2 hours every morning putting on lots of makeup, and I bet it's not even cruelty-free!

3) Say super mean & catty stuff! Celestabelleabethabelle called Wendy "Stretch," and told Candy that she was pretty, but not "TV pretty."
What the heck!

4) As it turns out, necks just taste like . . . horses' necks. Not good.

5) Way judgmental! The only quest Celestabelleabethabelle makes you go on is one to recover your self-esteem!

6) The only magical thing about Celestabelleabethabelle was her rainbow blood—which I discovered when I punched her in the face.

**WEAKNESS:** PUNCHING (IN THE FACE)

(ALSO: TEAMWORK)

(ALSO: GRENDA)

I'm very worried Bill might try to play tricks on Dipper's mind. In order to prevent this, I have decided to employ one of my old devices:

# The Mind Reader

I hope to encrypt his thoughts or "Bill-proof" his mind.

Stray thoughts I noticed in Dipper's head:

—"I'm itchy. Why am I always itchy? Will I be itchy forever?"

—"I hope 'Ghost Harassers' lasts another few seasons."

—"Stan needs to hide his magazine collection better."

—"I hope Ford's not looking too closely at these thoughts."

—"Try to think of nothing. Ugh, that was something!"

The procedure takes hours to complete, and when I fell asleep waiting, my clever nephew used the Mind Reader to see into my mind. My jumbled memories made him believe that I was still in cahoots with Bill, and he defended himself with Fiddleford's memory gun.

What a disaster! And the whole thing could've been avoided if I had just come clean about Bill. It's time that I tell Dipper everything, regardless of what he thinks of me afterward.

I've told Dipper my history with Bill, and to my great relief, he was very understanding. Luck seems to be on our side today! Mabel has returned with a large tuft of unicorn hair. We have circled the base of the Shack with it to create a . . .

# Mystical Barrier.

Although we were unable to "Bill-proof" Dipper's mind, this should make the Shack and anyone inside it impervious to Bill's power. After our latest misadventure, I realized it was time to tell Dipper everything I knew about Gravity Falls. I sat him down and told him to ask me any question he could think of about the town. No more secrets. His first question made me beam with pride:

# WHY IS GRAVITY FALLS SO WEIRD?

# The true theory of
# WEIRDNESS

I told Dipper that I'd spent my young adulthood obsessed with this question. Bill Cipher told me that the weirdness in town leaked in from another dimension—but this was a lie. Bill was simply trying to trick me into opening a door so he could claim Gravity Falls for himself.

The truth, I explained, was a bit stranger. To help Dipper understand, I borrowed Stanley's car, and we drove until we reached the town border of Gravity Falls. I pulled a bag of jellybeans out of my pocket and began to explain.

Everything in the universe is like a jelly bean—made of the same basic materials, varied in color and flavor, but all more or less conforming to an expected pattern. But every now and then, by chance, a bean comes out deformed

**ODD ONE OF THE BUNCH**

. . . odd . . . weird. I pulled an especially strange bean out to show him, and then dropped it and the rest of the bag at my feet.

The beans began to tumble downhill, but one bean, the deformed one, almost magically rolled backwards, UP the hill, right UP TO THE TOWN BORDER

Dipper's eyes widened. I could see him beginning to understand. Why had this one bean rolled uphill?

The reason? Gravity Falls is a . . .

# WEIRDNESS MAGNET!

Oddness is strangely, mysteriously drawn to this place, from misshapen jelly beans, to gnomes and fairies to dinosaurs, interdimensional tears, clones, crazy ex-presidents, even men with six fingers and boys with strange birthmarks. I explained that I felt in my bones that my arrival at this town, and perhaps Dipper's, too, was not an accident. That we were part of some greater fate the town had in store for us. "You and I are some of the strangest beans this town has ever seen, Dipper," I told him.

"Mason," he blurted out. He seemed shocked by what had come out of his mouth, and then deliberately repeated it. "My real name is Mason. Dipper is just a nickname. But everyone got used to it, and now it feels too late to tell everyone the truth. And it's kind of a dumb name anyway. Don't tell anyone."

I tussled his hair and smiled at him. "Your secret's safe with me, Mason." I said. "And I think it's a great name. The Masons are a great secret society, you know." He smiled. I realized how much he trusted me—and what a shame it was that he was leaving at the end of the summer. I have begun to form an idea . . .

# THE RIFT CONTAINMENT UNIT IS CRACKING!

*I suggested it would be a good time for Stan to take the kids on that road trip he's been talking about while I puzzle over this problem. If the unit breaks, all the madness of Bill's Nightmare Dimension will come spilling into ours!*

⟨cipher text, three lines⟩

In order to seal the rift for good, it is going to take an adhesive of unearthly strength. I must return to Crash Site Omega—although I suppose there's no longer any need for that coy nickname invented in my youth. Since my nephew has decided to share his secrets with me, then I shall share mine as well. As I referenced in Journal 2, there is an

# ENORMOUS EXTRATERRESTRIAL CRAFT

## buried under the valley of Gravity Falls.

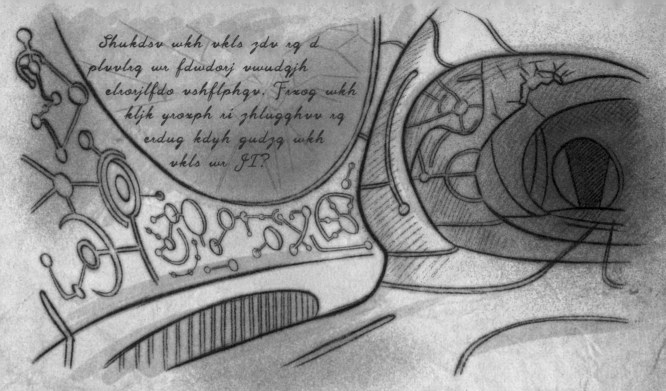

Shukdsv wkh vkls zdv rq d plvvlrq wr fdwdorj vwudqjh elrorjlfdo vshflphqv. Frxog wkh kljk yroxph ri zhlugqhvv rq erdug kdyh gudzq wkh vkls wr JT?

The enormous scale of the entire interior would be impossible to capture on these pages. But here are a few of the more intriguing aspects of the ship . . .

In my long, dimension-hopping life, I've only encountered one creature that fits this skeleton shape: the Pan-Dimensional Beings of Trilazzzz Beta. Since they exist in 7 to 11 dimensions at once, they have a horrible sense of direction. No wonder the ship crashed.

A ship this big has not only climate control, but also actual full-blown weather. I spotted levers for sunshine, rain, and even snow.

Not sure what the tornado button is for. . . . Maybe a quick way to wipe out the crew in case of a mutiny?

WEATHER CONTROLS

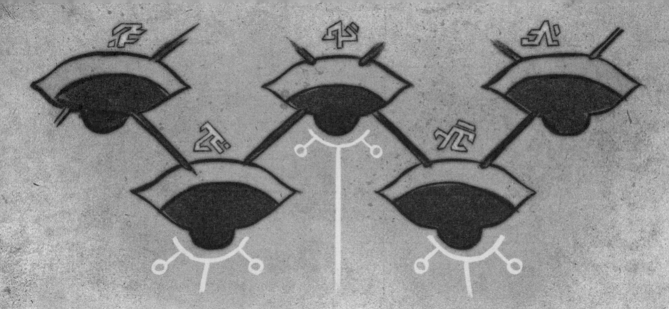

Having an alien ship under the town has caused many odd disturbances. Stoplights that don't work properly. Electrical interference. Sick livestock. And occasional stories of vehicles being magnetically hurled off roads.

A heavily guarded biological containment center apparently once housed eggs and larvae of other species discovered on alien worlds. Although judging by the claw marks and shattered glass, it seemed likely something escaped. ~~Something seemed very familiar about this.~~ . . .

Of course, I doubt that I will have time to show any of this to Dipper on his first trip to CSO. We'll need to retrieve Alien Adhesive, and I'm thinking of discussing my apprenticeship offer with him this afternoon. If luck is with us, the security system is still defunct. . . .

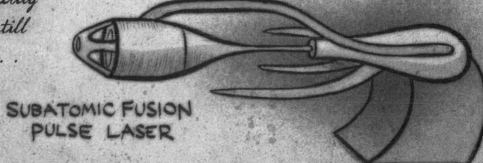

SUBATOMIC FUSION
PULSE LASER

# THE WORST HAS HAPPENED! BILL HAS BEEN LET LOOSE IN OUR WORLD!

    I don't know who got hold of the rift or who Bill deceived, but right now it does not matter. There is very little time to write, but I feel it necessary to quickly summarize our plan in case we fail and it falls to others to fight this beast.

    I only have one charge left on my Quantum Destabilizer, the weapon that required Parallel Fiddleford's brilliance to complete. If all goes according to plan, we will use it to destroy Bill. It should transform him into a weirdness black hole, and suck all the strangeness from the Nightmare Realm out of our own world.

But only a direct hit to the center of his body will work!!

I pray that if we fail, others will take up this fight. The fate of the world, the fate of the entire universe, depends on it!!! This may be the last time that I write in this journal, or any journal, ever again. I know I have made many mistakes in my life, but I pray that I can finally make things right.

# August 25,

Dipper here! I can't believe I'm holding this book in my hands. I saw Bill burn all 3 journals right in front of me!! But this morning, Soos found the journals lying in the woods, unharmed. Apparently, defeating Bill didn't just de-weird the town, it also restored many of the things he destroyed—including the journals!

But I'm getting ahead of myself again. Let me start over:

1) Bill came out of a rip in the sky and took over Gravity Falls.

2) Bill captured Ford and turned him to gold.

3) Bill tried to trap Mabel in a mind prison, and blew up Time Baby. (I wonder what ever happened to Blendin. . . . I hope he's okay.)

4) The town banded together to save Ford and defeat Bill, and it was McGucket who figured out how. True, his solution to every problem is "Build a giant robot!", but this time he was on OUR side!

I don't know if he's gotten saner or crazier after the events of Weirdmageddon, but either way, he's become a bona fide hero—and made the rest of us heroes in the process. No one else could have dreamed up . . .

# THE SHACKTRON!

The robot's fighting style was inspired by Soos's favorite anime, "Neon Crisis Revelations Angry Cute Girl: Annihilation." He kept requesting giving the robot a "Gun-Sword," but we told him that's . . . not a thing.

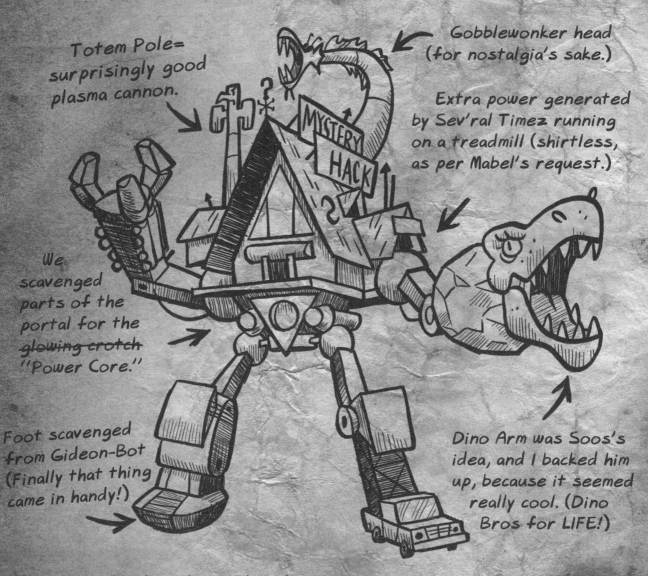

Totem Pole= surprisingly good plasma cannon.

Gobblewonker head (for nostalgia's sake.)

Extra power generated by Sev'ral Timez running on a treadmill (shirtless, as per Mabel's request.)

We scavenged parts of the portal for the ~~glowing crotch~~ "Power Core."

Foot scavenged from Gideon-Bot (Finally that thing came in handy!)

Dino Arm was Soos's idea, and I backed him up, because it seemed really cool. (Dino Bros for LIFE!)

MYSTERY HACK

While Candy and Grenda led the Shacktron into battle, our rescue team parachuted inside the Fearamid and unfroze Ford. He told us that we all had a crucial role to play as part of . . .

# The ZODIAC

According to Ford, this was a prophecy found painted in the same cave where he originally summoned Bill. Ford had never believed the legend before (apparently he couldn't believe that saving the world involved so much getting along with others), but he thought it was finally worth a try.

We seemed to have all the right people—amazingly it even included past enemies, like Pacifica, Gideon, & Robbie. (In retrospect, it's pretty good we ended up getting over our grudges with those three.)

Unfortunately, Stan could not get over all his "big issues" with Ford long enough to join hands, so the whole thing fizzled out and Bill attacked us!

We still have no idea what would have happened if we had completed the Zodiac's prophecy! Soos imagines that the Zodiac would have given us all "radness powers." Somehow I doubt that this is what the ancients had in mind.

↖ Unlikely

In the end, it turned out to be Grunkle Stan who saved us all—by erasing his own mind, with Bill inside. When Mabel and I found out what had happened, I think both of us were too shocked to believe it. And luckily, Mabel refused to believe it! After tearfully showing Grunkle Stan her scrapbook, she managed to spark bits of Stan's mind back to life—and began recovering his memory bit by bit!

It turns out that the memory ray's effects can be undone through exposure to important images and people from your past (in the same way that McGucket began his road to recovery when he saw the tape of himself as a young inventor). The reason Stan recovered so much faster is that we began recovery while the erasure was still fresh—less than an hour after initial contact.

Still, it's taken about a week of intensive scrapbook therapy to get Stan fully back to himself. While the townsfolk and McGucket helped rebuild the Shack, Ford, Mabel, & I have been spending almost every minute with Stan, retelling him his life story, feeding him his favorite foods (toffee peanuts & bacon), playing songs from when he was in high school, and driving him through town to revisit every spot he's ever seen (and every person he's ever swindled.) We've even read his favorite terrible jokes from his joke book to him, and he remembers every punch line.

Ford's been working at it the hardest. Seeing Stan's memory erased is the only time any of us have ever seen Ford cry. There have been several nights we've found that Ford has fallen asleep on the couch next to Stan, exhausted from a marathon of describing their childhoods together—and from apologizing for his mistakes.

Ford even found an old film reel of them as kids, which he amazingly saved all these years. There are clips of them playing on the beach, goofing around at the dinner table and pawn shop, and dressing as explorers in oversized helmets trying to find the "Jersey Devil."

Stan & Ford are downstairs in the living room watching the home movies right now. As much as we want to watch too, we think this is something they should do on their own. They've earned it.

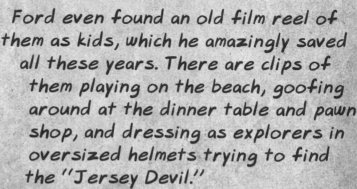

August 27,

I'll admit, I've been geeking out hard-core the last couple of days over having all 3 journals in my possession. Not only did defeating Bill fix the journals, but it turns out that it also restored pages that had long since been burned or ripped out. There's countless pages in here that I never saw before, things I would have killed to know earlier in the summer. The journals even SMELL better. (Slightly less like millipedes!)

Part of me wants to keep the journals forever as a birthday gift to myself, but I know I've got to tell Ford about them. They belong to him. I just hope he won't be mad that I've kept them to myself this long.

Besides, there's no way I could forget the strange creatures and events we've both written about here. This journal was my guide to someone else's adventure—and now it's time I start my own.

I've even started my own journal to take back to California. (Do you like the cover?) I told Ford that I wouldn't be taking his apprenticeship, and he completely understood. Apparently he's thinking of asking someone else to be his new partner in crime. (And I think we both know someone who's <u>great</u> at crime.)

I'll never forget the most amazing summer of my life or the family and friends who made it that way—and I'll never forget the book that first opened my eyes to the mysteries of the universe.

This is ~~M~~ Dipper Pines, signing off for the final time.

(Don't be mad, Grunkle Ford!!)

My grandnephew's fears are unfounded. All I feel toward him is love and pride. He is a wiser man at ~~twelve~~ thirteen than I was at thirty. He has an incredible future ahead of him—one in which he will hopefully avoid repeating my terrible errors.

Looking back on my lifetime of catastrophic mistakes, I realize one great pattern in all my follies. I thought being a great man meant being <u>alone</u>. Apart from the crowd. I bristled at the idea of sharing my accomplishments with anyone. I shunned my brother for one dumb mistake, and I shunned Fiddleford for having the sense to try to stop me from dooming the world.

Even when I was given a second chance, I still held others at a distance. If I had been able to widen my circle of trust . . . if I had believed in the Zodiac's prophecy sooner . . . we might have gathered everyone together and banished Bill before he was able to strike. I just couldn't get over the idea of myself as the lone hero . . . and it was Stanley who paid the price.

"Trust No One."
What an absurd and paranoid idea. Trust shouldn't be given unconditionally, but it should be given a chance to be earned. There is strength in having the humility to work with and sacrifice for others—a strength I now realize was in my brother all along.

Stanley Pines was the man who saved the world, not me. I spent so long thinking he was a selfish jerk, and he turned out to be the most selfless man I've ever met in any dimension. If I'm totally honest, I must admit that he's a hero and I'm . . . a hero's brother.
And I'm okay with that.
Thank goodness he is recovering his wonderfully twisted mind. And I vow to spend the rest of my days making things right between us . . .
   If only he gives
       me a chance.

STAN O' WAR

# There was someone else I needed to make amends to . . .
# my old partner, Fiddleford McGucket.

We reunited during Weirdmaggedon, but it was far too brief, so after things calmed down, I went to visit him. Dipper had warned me about Fiddleford's uneven mental state, but when I saw that he was living at the dump, it became clear how deeply I had hurt this man that I had once held so dear.

He was overjoyed to see me, and we spent hours talking. He was fascinated by my tales of the multiverse, and his probing questions made it clear that his excellent mind had recovered most of its enormous capacity. My feelings of guilt returned when the conversation turned to the subject of his self-induced memory loss, but I dismissed my attempts to apologize. Not only is this man's mind superior to mine, but he has one of the biggest hearts I've ever seen.

I have found one way to try to make things up to him. During my visit, I discovered a large trove of blueprints. F dismissed them as "doodles," but in truth they are an amazing array of futuristic machines the likes of which I have never seen. I _insisted_ that he submit these plans to the U.S. government. I believe the royalties will allow him to significantly upgrade his living arrangements. (And possibly wear shoes for the first time in 30 years.)

We also talked about our family members—and how his had turned their backs on him when he lost his mind. I encouraged him to reach out to them. No matter how hard it is, everyone deserves a chance at having a family. Amazing that it took me so long to understand this.

Before I left, Fiddleford insisted that I listen to him play the banjo. I could have sworn that as he joyfully played, I could see the age lift off his face, and see the Fiddleford who had been my friend so many years ago.

I bid him good-bye for then—but I know we will have much to discuss in the future. I also noticed that the Cubic's Cube on his desk was perfectly completed—and for once I decided not to disturb it.

# August 29,

Gravity Falls is back to normal (at least, as normal as things get in this place). And although unusual phenomena are concentrated here, they are not confined to this location. There is a whole world out there that needs to be protected—and based on some strange signals I've seen in the Arctic Ocean, I think a new adventure might be right on the horizon.

When Stanley and I were kids, we would often read tales of the Sibling Brothers—about two boys who dedicated their lives to exploring mysteries together. (For the record: The butler stole the capers. OBVIOUSLY.) With a new anomaly to investigate, I've been thinking about those tales more and more lately.